The Misadventures of SALEM HYDE

3

DISCARD

Cookie Catastrophe

Frank Cammuso

AMULET BOOKS
NEW YORK

Hardcover ISBN: 978-1-4197-1198-5
Paperback ISBN: 978-1-4197-1199-2

Text and illustrations copyright © 2014 Frank Cammuso
Book design by Frank Cammuso and Sara Corbett

Printed and bound in China
10 9 8 7 6 5 4 3 2 1

Amulet Books are available at special discounts when purchased in quantity for premiums and promotions as well as fundraising or educational use. Special editions can also be created to specification. For details, contact specialsales@abramsbooks.com or the address below.

THE ART OF BOOKS SINCE 1949
115 West 18th Street
New York, NY 10011
www.abramsbooks.com

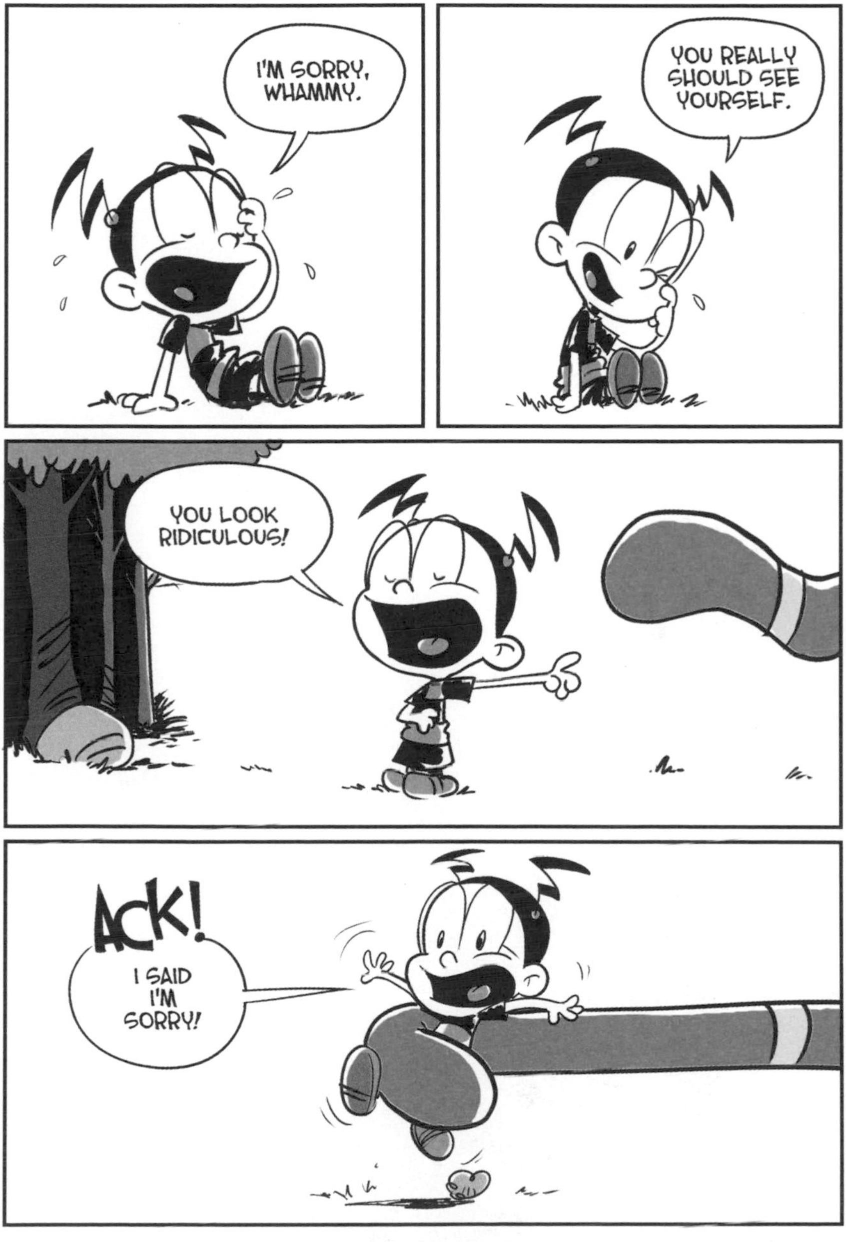
I'M SORRY, WHAMMY.
YOU REALLY SHOULD SEE YOURSELF.
YOU LOOK RIDICULOUS!
ACK!
I SAID I'M SORRY!

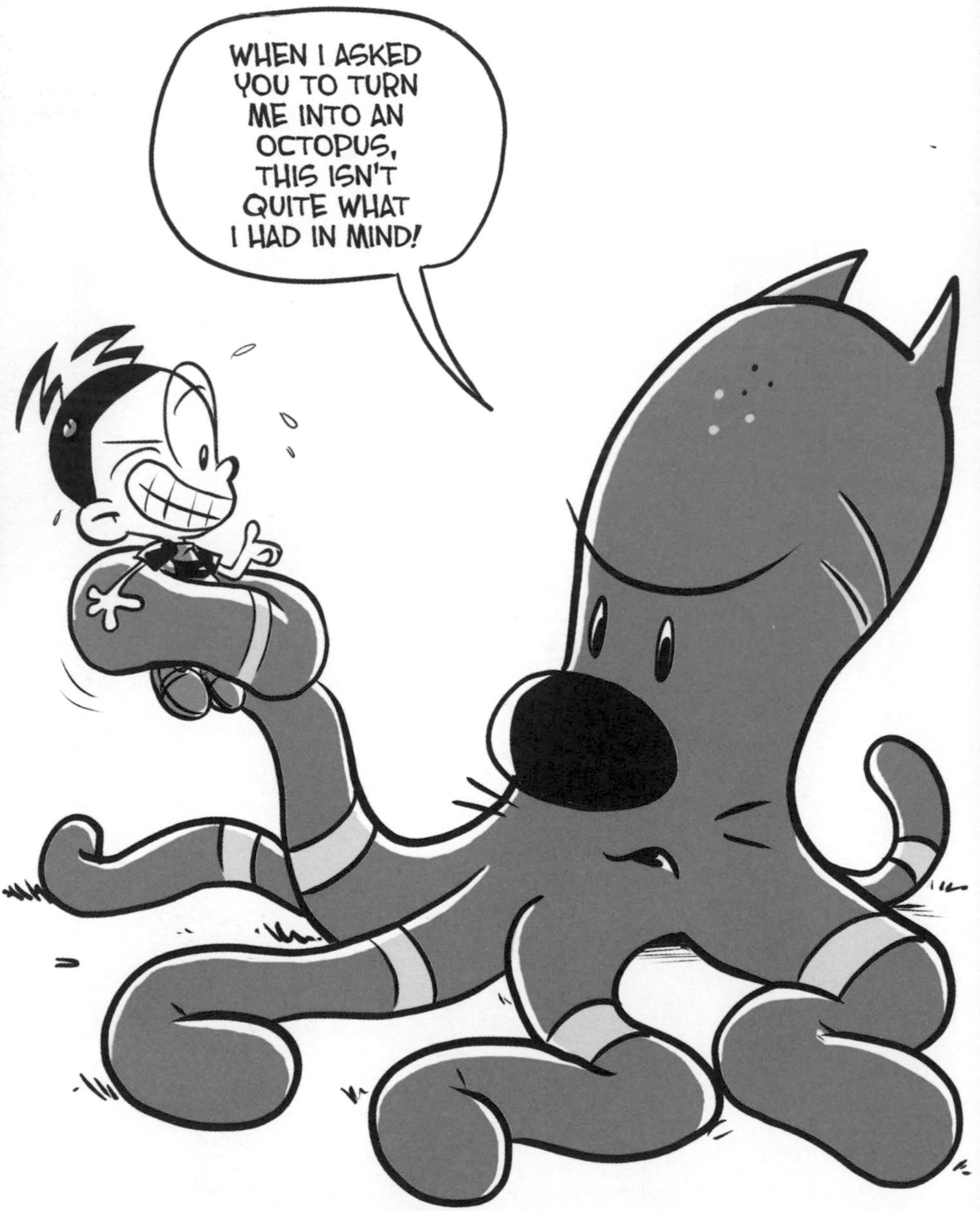
WHEN I ASKED YOU TO TURN ME INTO AN OCTOPUS, THIS ISN'T QUITE WHAT I HAD IN MIND!

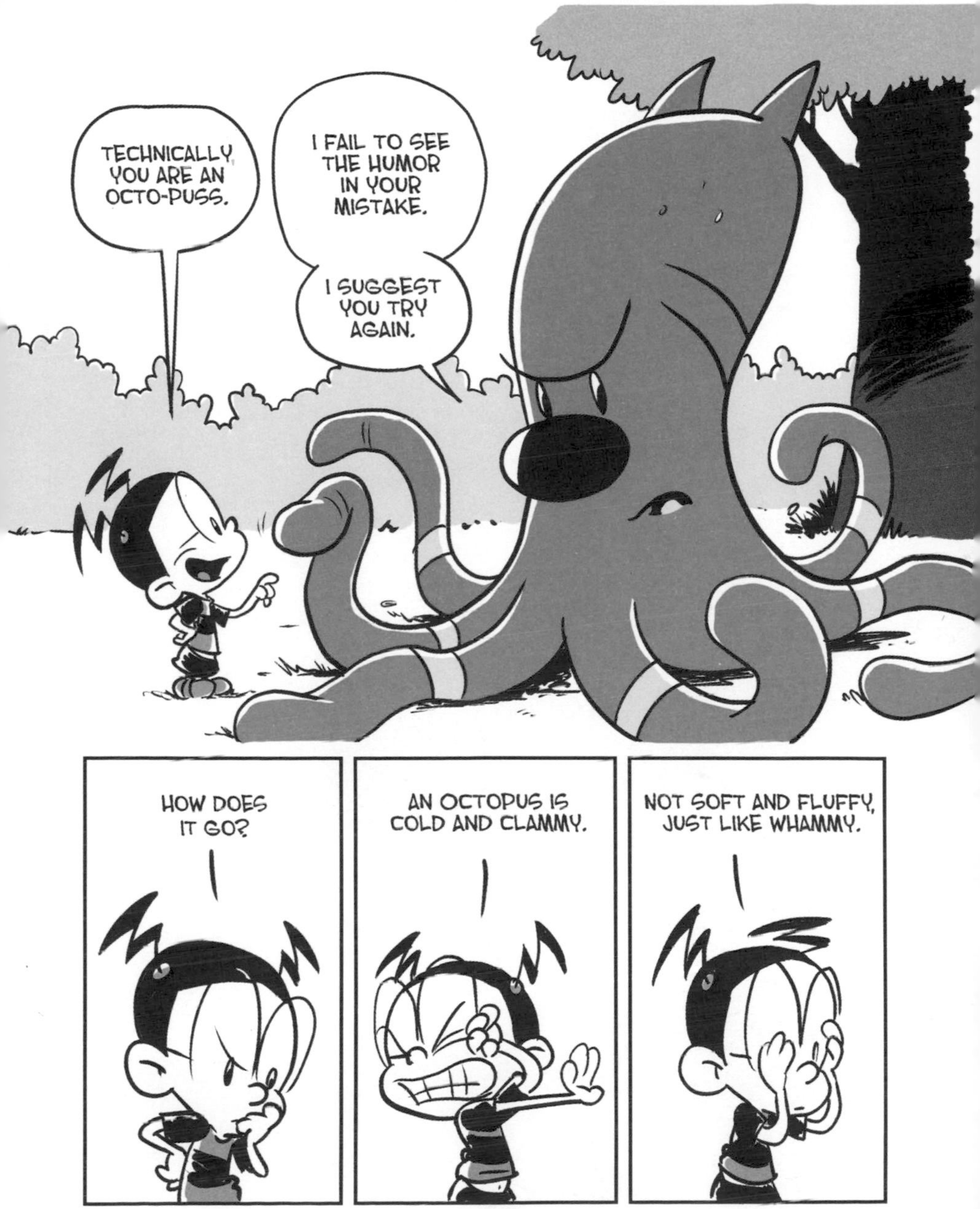
TECHNICALLY YOU ARE AN OCTO-PUSS.
I FAIL TO SEE THE HUMOR IN YOUR MISTAKE.
I SUGGEST YOU TRY AGAIN.
HOW DOES IT GO?
AN OCTOPUS IS COLD AND CLAMMY.
NOT SOFT AND FLUFFY, JUST LIKE WHAMMY.

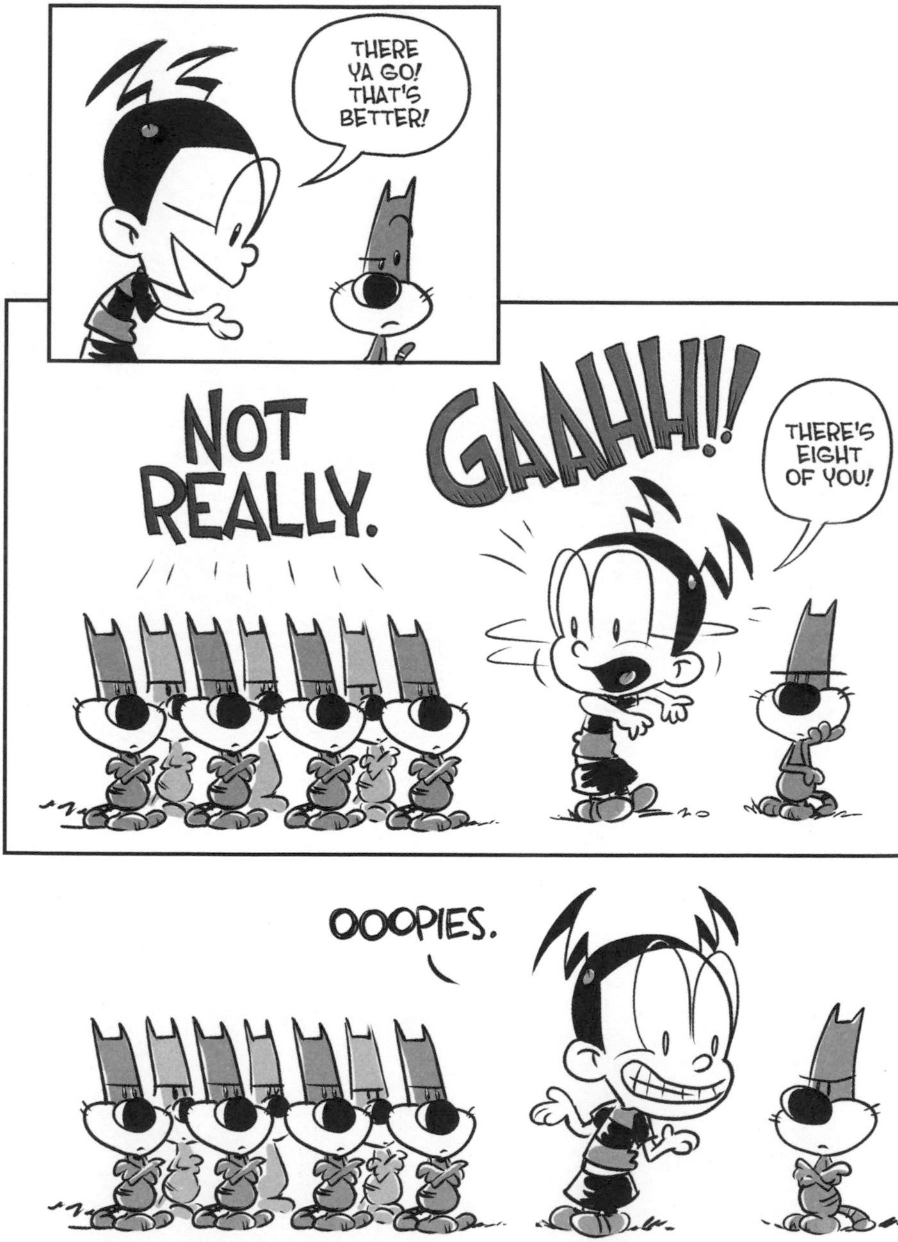
THERE YA GO! THAT'S BETTER!
NOT REALLY.
GAAHH!!
THERE'S EIGHT OF YOU!
OOOPIES.

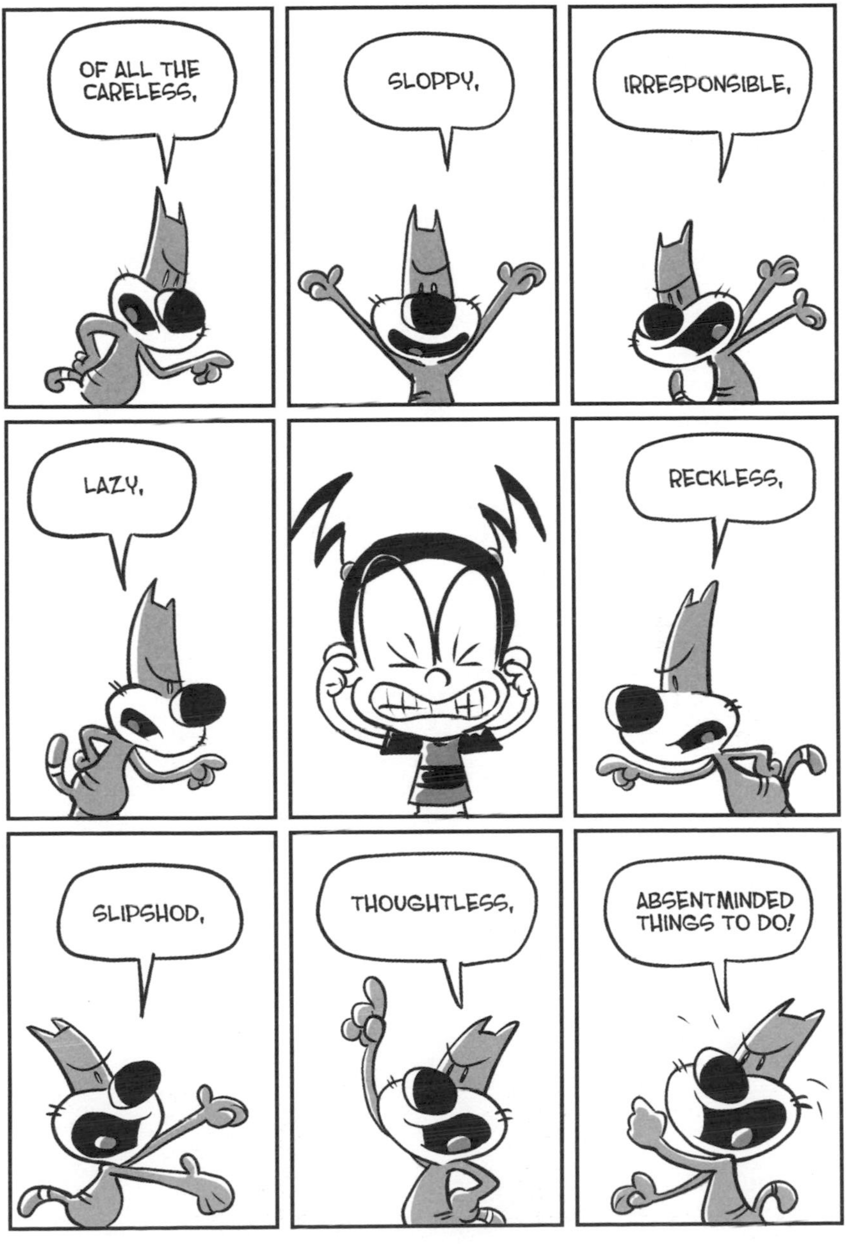
OF ALL THE CARELESS,
SLOPPY,
IRRESPONSIBLE,
LAZY,
RECKLESS,
SLIPSHOD,
THOUGHTLESS,
ABSENTMINDED THINGS TO DO!

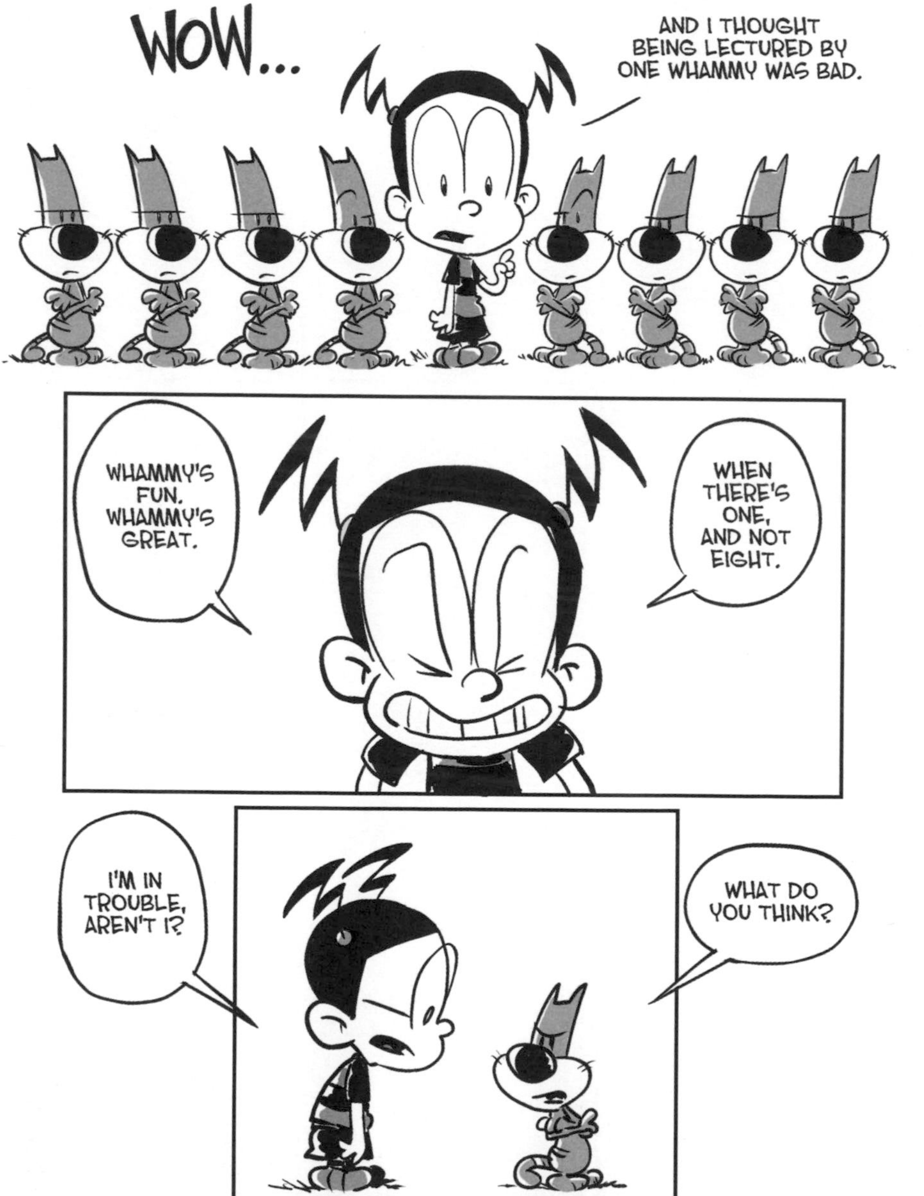
WOW...
AND I THOUGHT BEING LECTURED BY ONE WHAMMY WAS BAD.
WHAMMY'S FUN. WHAMMY'S GREAT.
WHEN THERE'S ONE, AND NOT EIGHT.
I'M IN TROUBLE, AREN'T I?
WHAT DO YOU THINK?

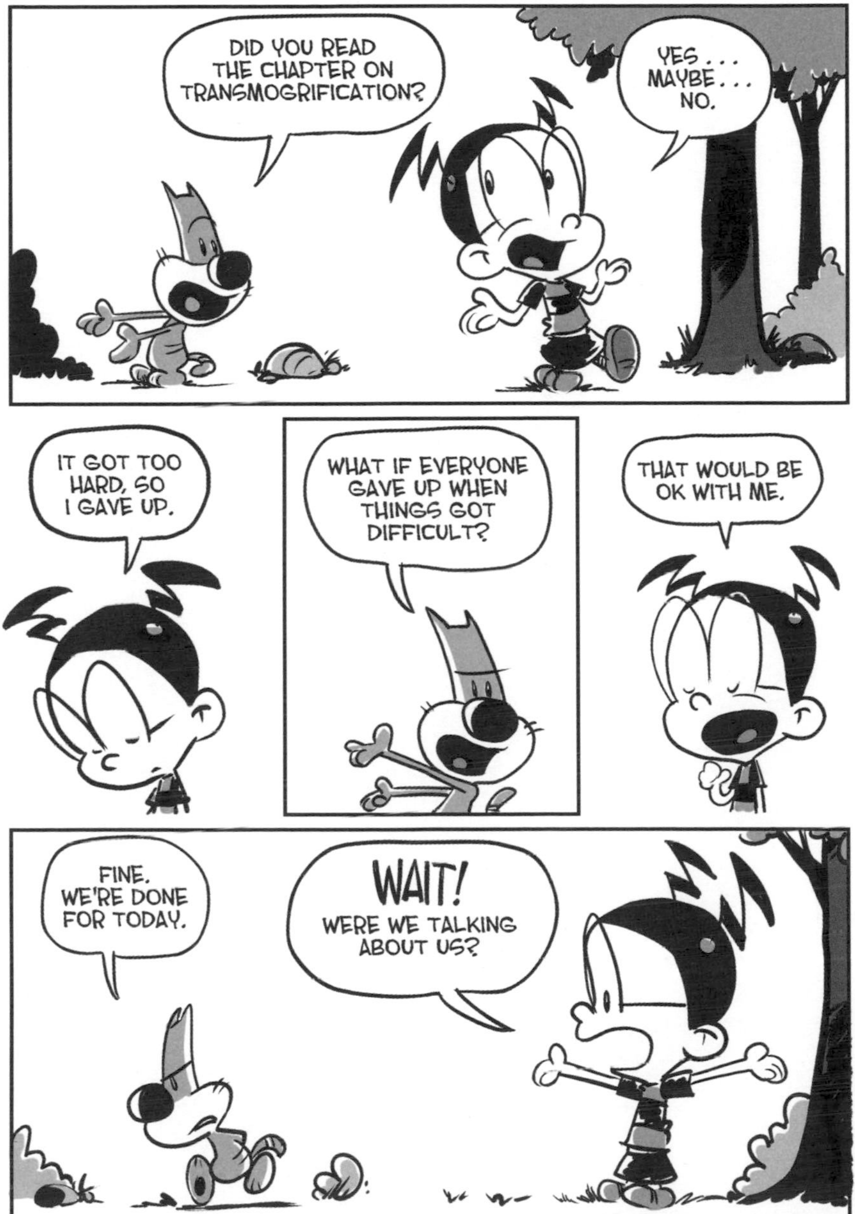
DID YOU READ THE CHAPTER ON TRANSMOGRIFICATION?
YES . . . MAYBE . . . NO.
IT GOT TOO HARD, SO I GAVE UP.
WHAT IF EVERYONE GAVE UP WHEN THINGS GOT DIFFICULT?
THAT WOULD BE OK WITH ME.
FINE. WE'RE DONE FOR TODAY.
WAIT! WERE WE TALKING ABOUT US?

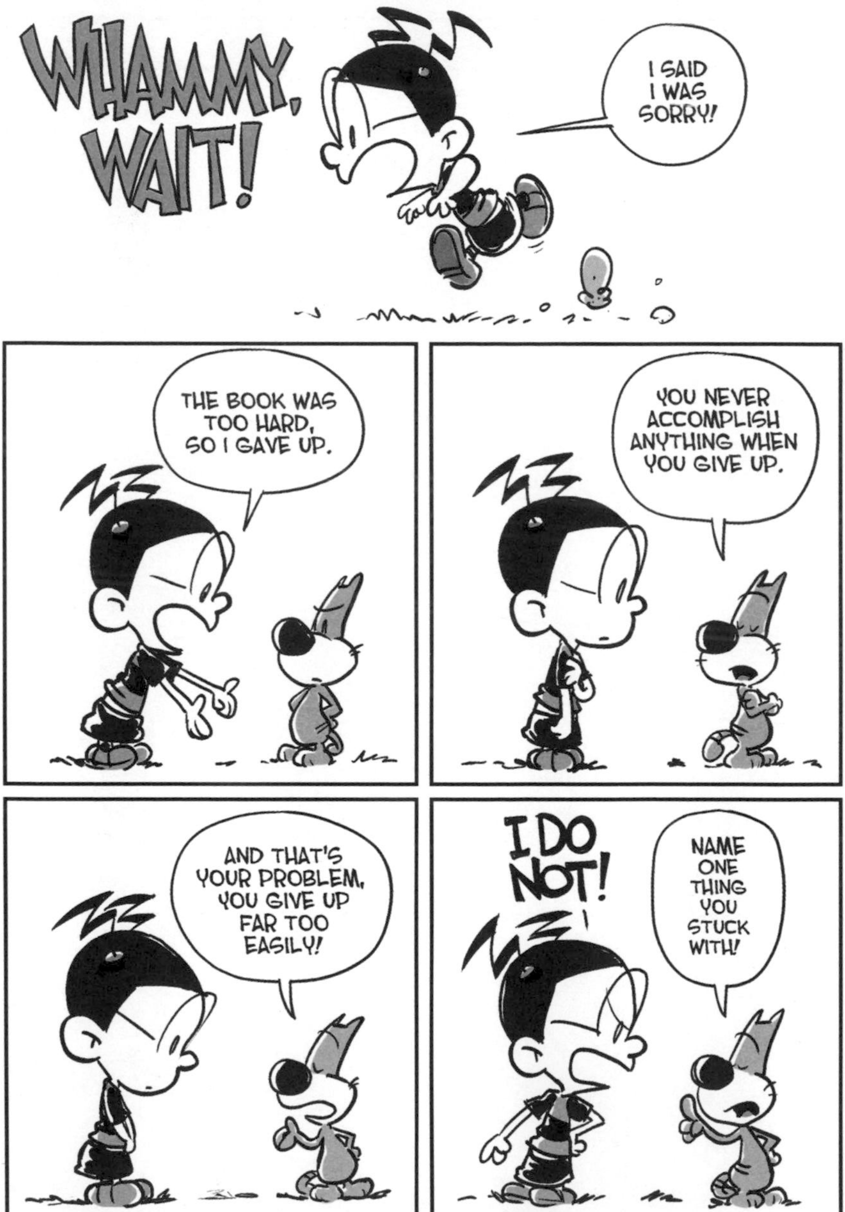
WHAMMY, WAIT!
I SAID I WAS SORRY!
THE BOOK WAS TOO HARD, SO I GAVE UP.
YOU NEVER ACCOMPLISH ANYTHING WHEN YOU GIVE UP.
AND THAT'S YOUR PROBLEM, YOU GIVE UP FAR TOO EASILY!
I DO NOT!
NAME ONE THING YOU STUCK WITH!

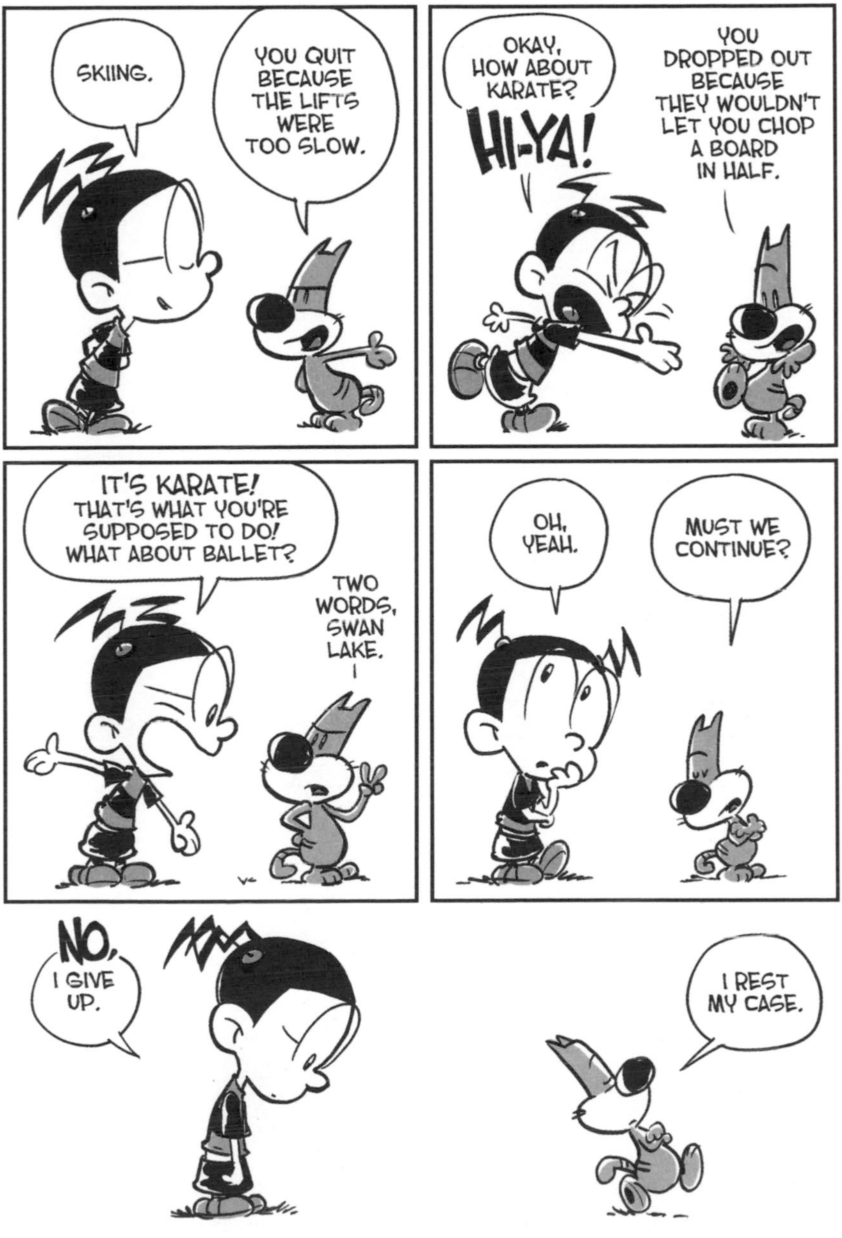
SKIING.
YOU QUIT BECAUSE THE LIFTS WERE TOO SLOW.
OKAY, HOW ABOUT KARATE?
HI-YA!
YOU DROPPED OUT BECAUSE THEY WOULDN'T LET YOU CHOP A BOARD IN HALF.
IT'S KARATE! THAT'S WHAT YOU'RE SUPPOSED TO DO! WHAT ABOUT BALLET?
TWO WORDS, SWAN LAKE.
OH, YEAH.
MUST WE CONTINUE?
NO, I GIVE UP.
I REST MY CASE.

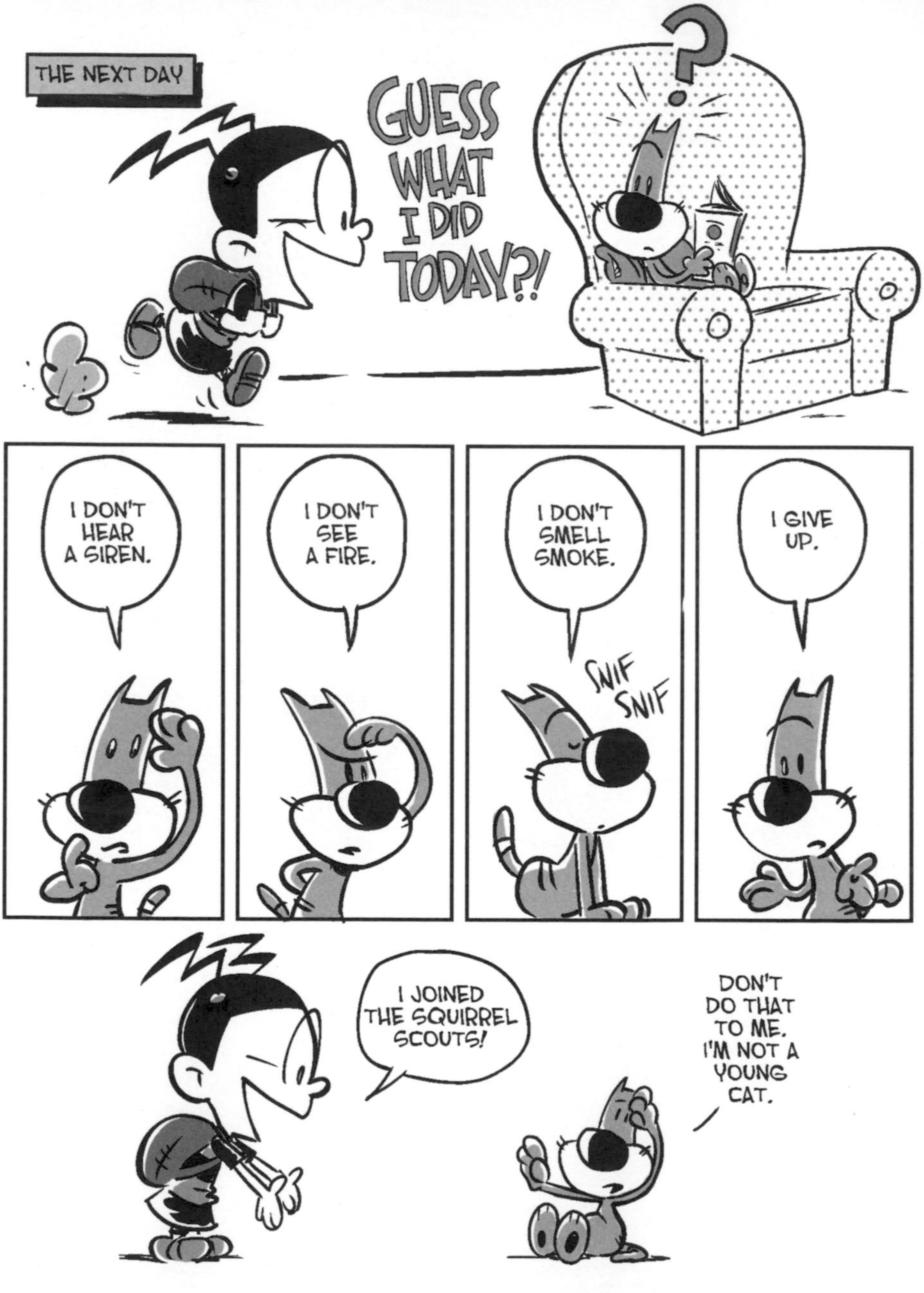
THE NEXT DAY
GUESS WHAT I DID TODAY?!
?
I DON'T HEAR A SIREN.
I DON'T SEE A FIRE.
I DON'T SMELL SMOKE.
SNIF SNIF
I GIVE UP.
I JOINED THE SQUIRREL SCOUTS!
DON'T DO THAT TO ME. I'M NOT A YOUNG CAT.

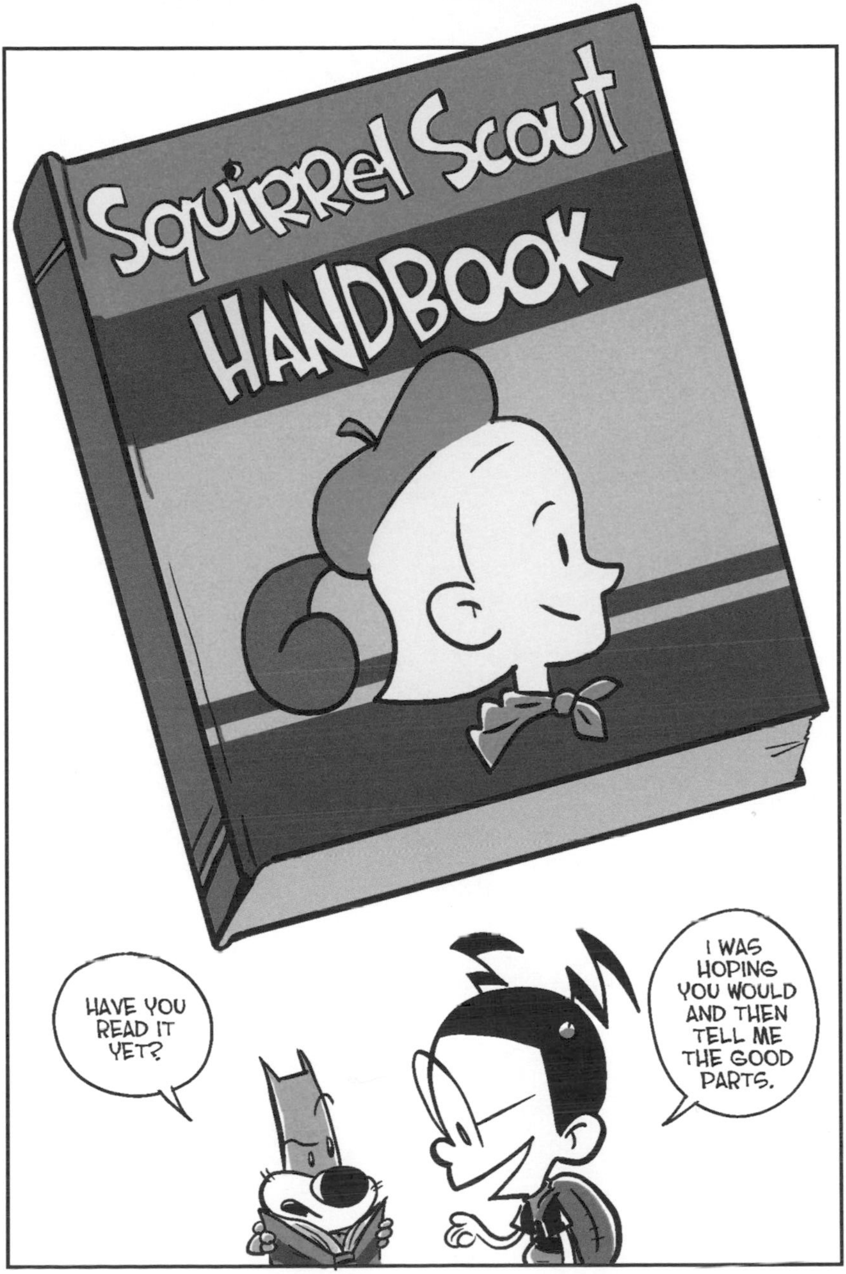
Squirrel Scout
HANDBOOK
HAVE YOU READ IT YET?
I WAS HOPING YOU WOULD AND THEN TELL ME THE GOOD PARTS.

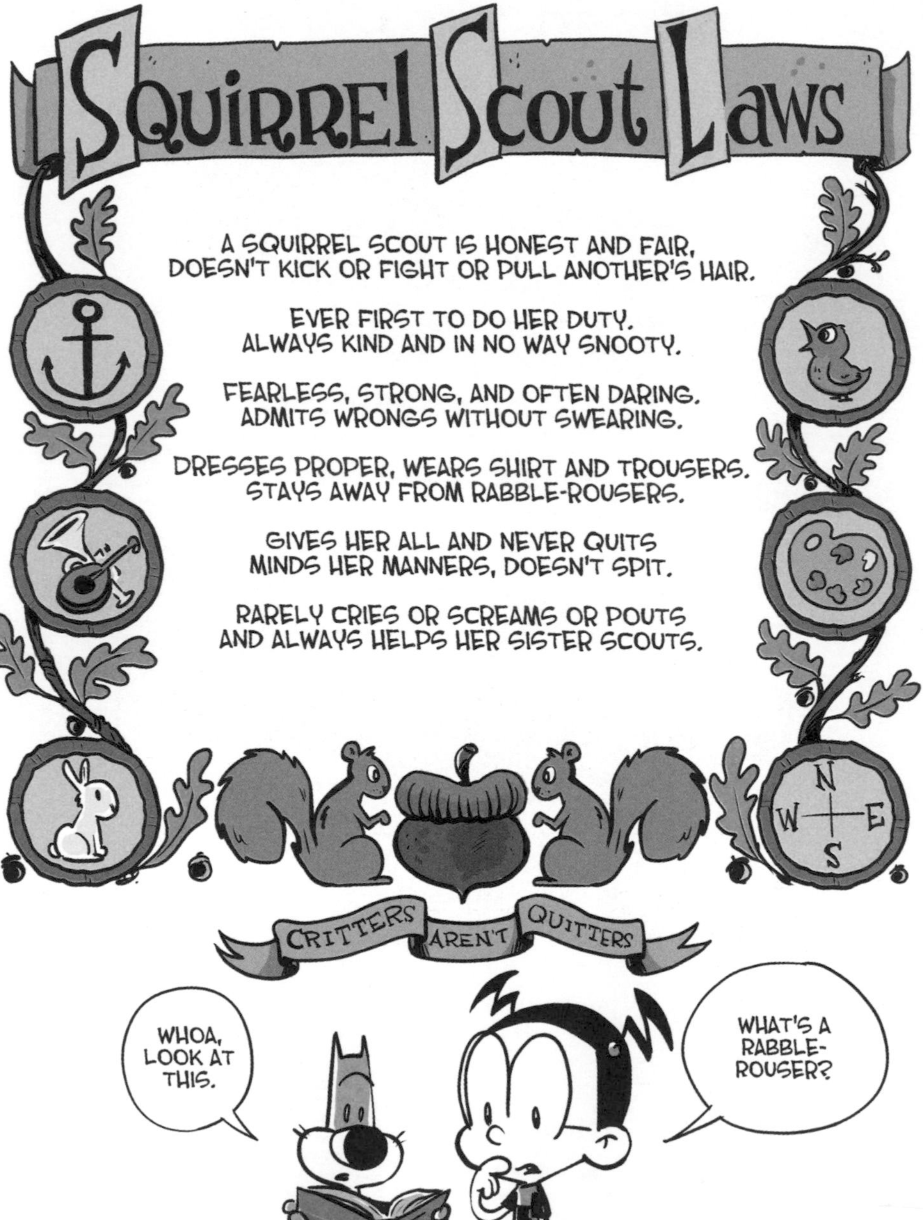

SQUIRREL SCOUT LAWS
A SQUIRREL SCOUT IS HONEST AND FAIR,
DOESN'T KICK OR FIGHT OR PULL ANOTHER'S HAIR.
EVER FIRST TO DO HER DUTY.
ALWAYS KIND AND IN NO WAY SNOOTY.
FEARLESS, STRONG, AND OFTEN DARING.
ADMITS WRONGS WITHOUT SWEARING.
DRESSES PROPER, WEARS SHIRT AND TROUSERS.
STAYS AWAY FROM RABBLE-ROUSERS.
GIVES HER ALL AND NEVER QUITS
MINDS HER MANNERS, DOESN'T SPIT.
RARELY CRIES OR SCREAMS OR POUTS
AND ALWAYS HELPS HER SISTER SCOUTS.
N
W
E
S
CRITTERS AREN'T QUITTERS
WHOA, LOOK AT THIS.
WHAT'S A RABBLE-ROUSER?

PART 1
BECOMING A Squirrel Scout

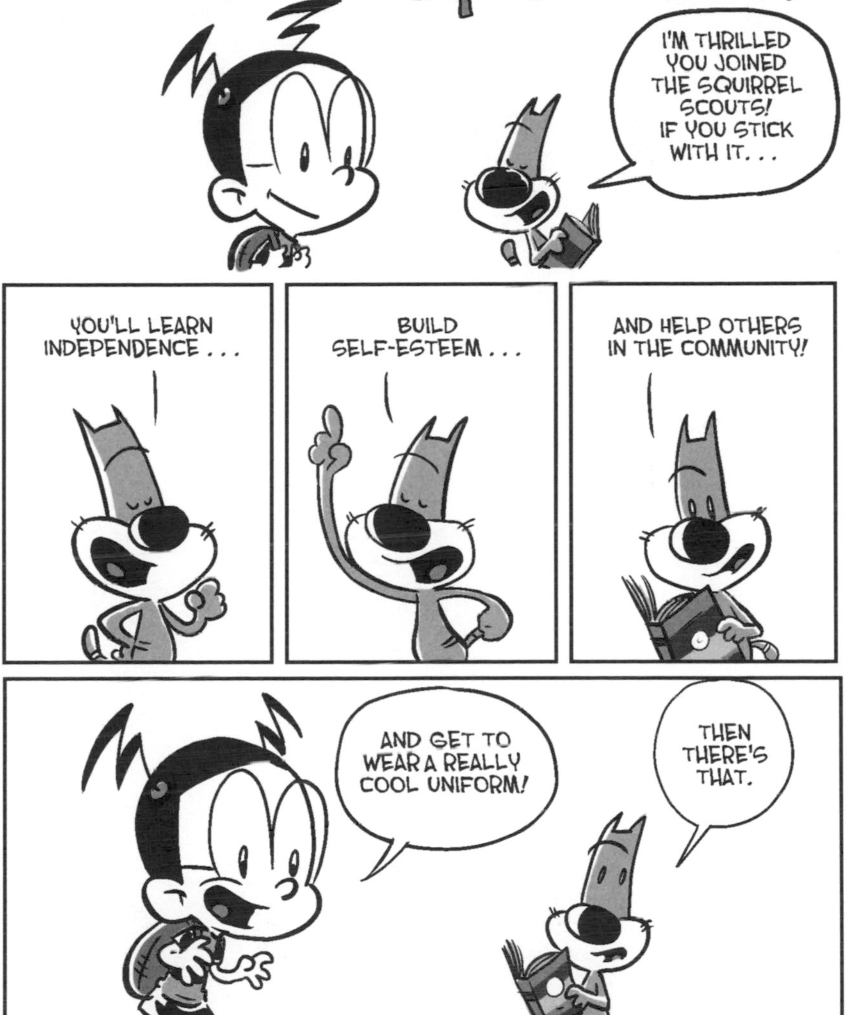
I'M THRILLED YOU JOINED THE SQUIRREL SCOUTS! IF YOU STICK WITH IT. . .
YOU'LL LEARN INDEPENDENCE . . .
BUILD SELF-ESTEEM . . .
AND HELP OTHERS IN THE COMMUNITY!
AND GET TO WEAR A REALLY COOL UNIFORM!
THEN THERE'S THAT.

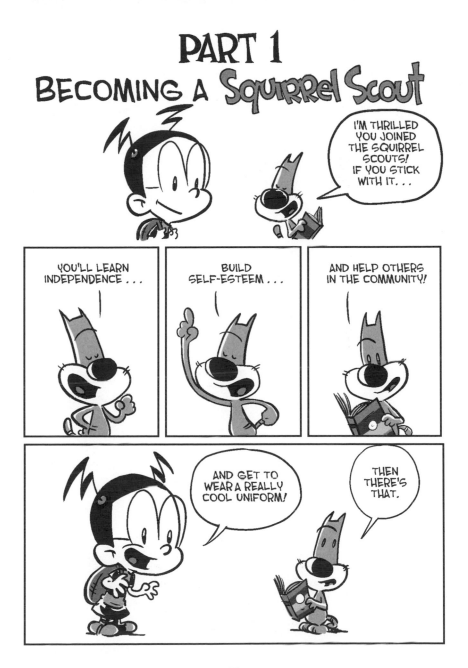

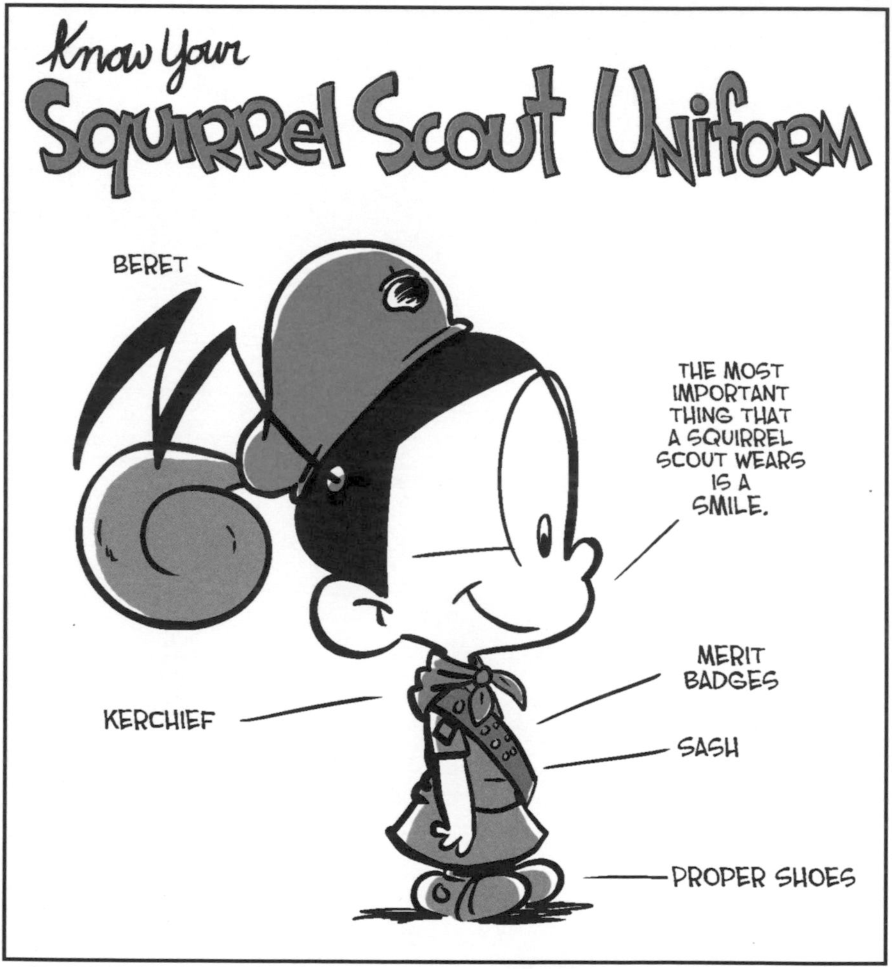
Know Your
Squirrel Scout Uniform
BERET
THE MOST IMPORTANT THING THAT A SQUIRREL SCOUT WEARS IS A SMILE.
MERIT BADGES
KERCHIEF
SASH
PROPER SHOES

SAMPLE MERIT BADGES

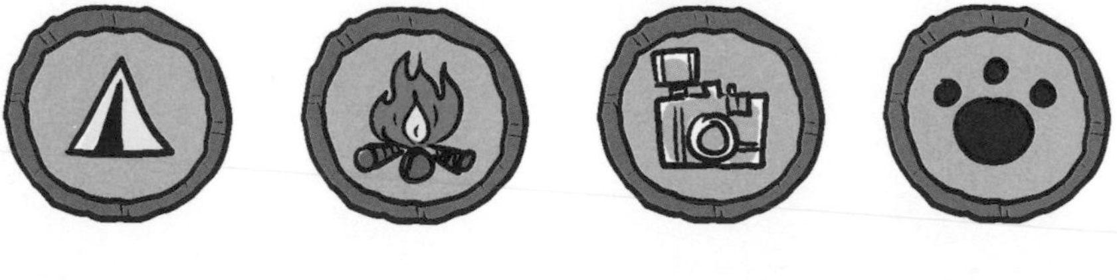

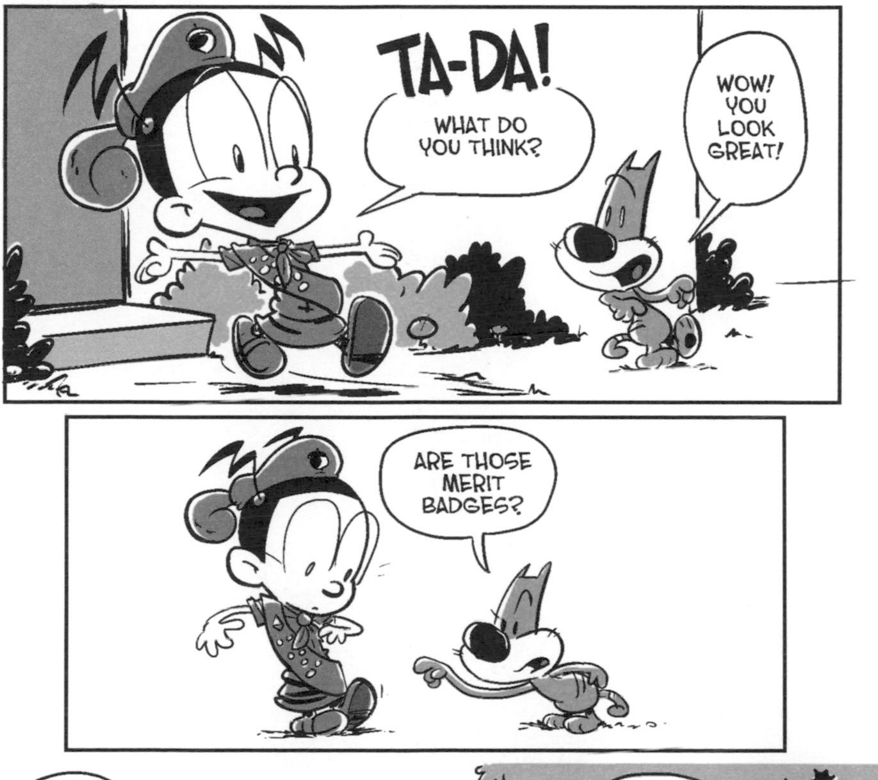
TA-DA!
WHAT DO YOU THINK?
WOW! YOU LOOK GREAT!
ARE THOSE MERIT BADGES?
NO, THEY'RE CRACKERS, IN CASE I GET HUNGRY.
CRUNCH
CRUNCH
BE PREPARED.

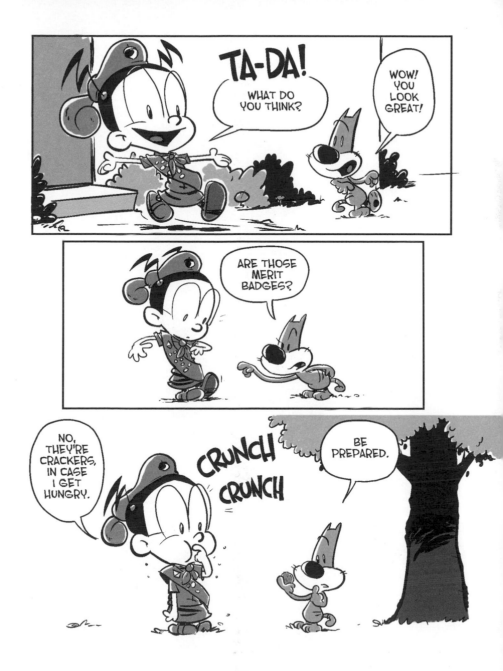

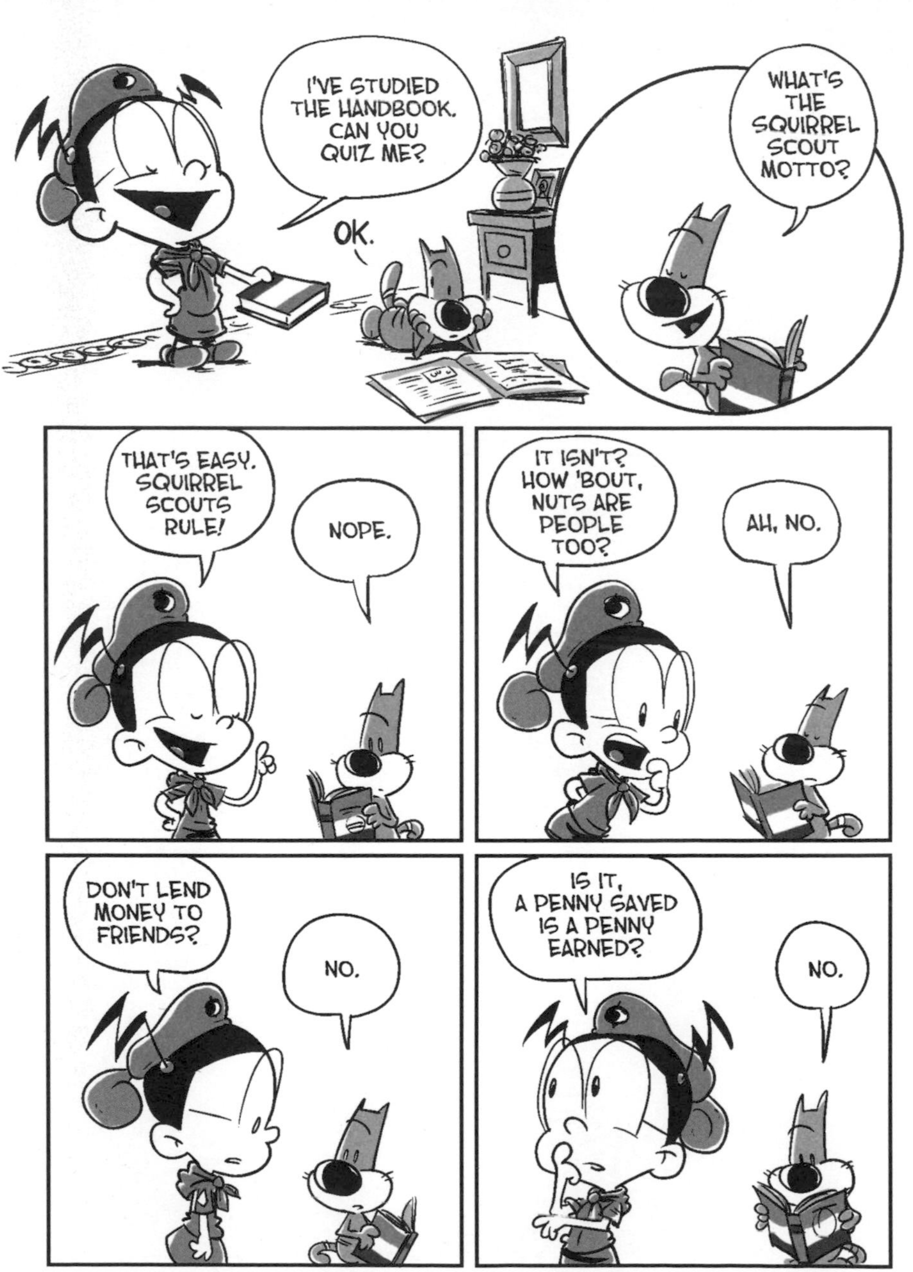
I'VE STUDIED THE HANDBOOK. CAN YOU QUIZ ME?
OK.
WHAT'S THE SQUIRREL SCOUT MOTTO?
THAT'S EASY. SQUIRREL SCOUTS RULE!
NOPE.
IT ISN'T? HOW 'BOUT, NUTS ARE PEOPLE TOO?
AH, NO.
DON'T LEND MONEY TO FRIENDS?
NO.
IS IT, A PENNY SAVED IS A PENNY EARNED?
NO.

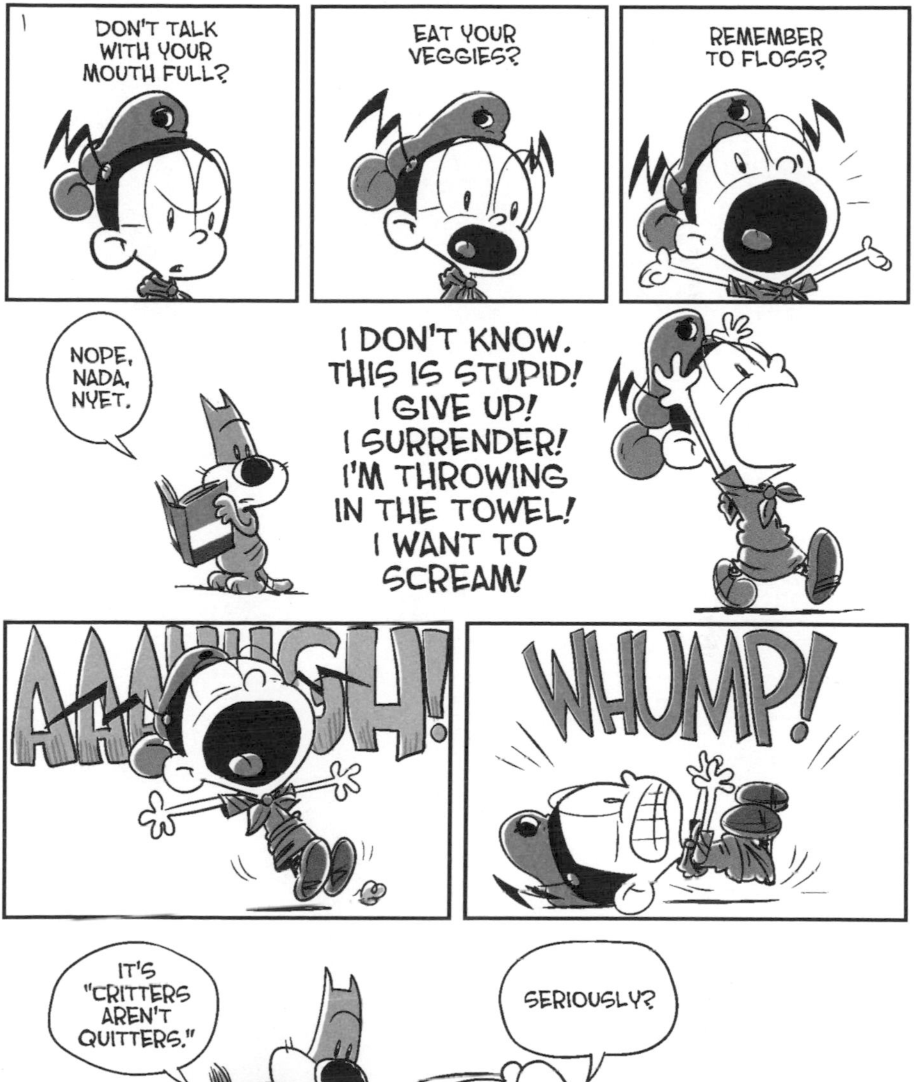
DON'T TALK WITH YOUR MOUTH FULL?
EAT YOUR VEGGIES?
REMEMBER TO FLOSS?
NOPE, NADA, NYET.
I DON'T KNOW. THIS IS STUPID! I GIVE UP! I SURRENDER! I'M THROWING IN THE TOWEL! I WANT TO SCREAM!
AAAUGH!
WHUMP!
IT'S "CRITTERS AREN'T QUITTERS."
SERIOUSLY?

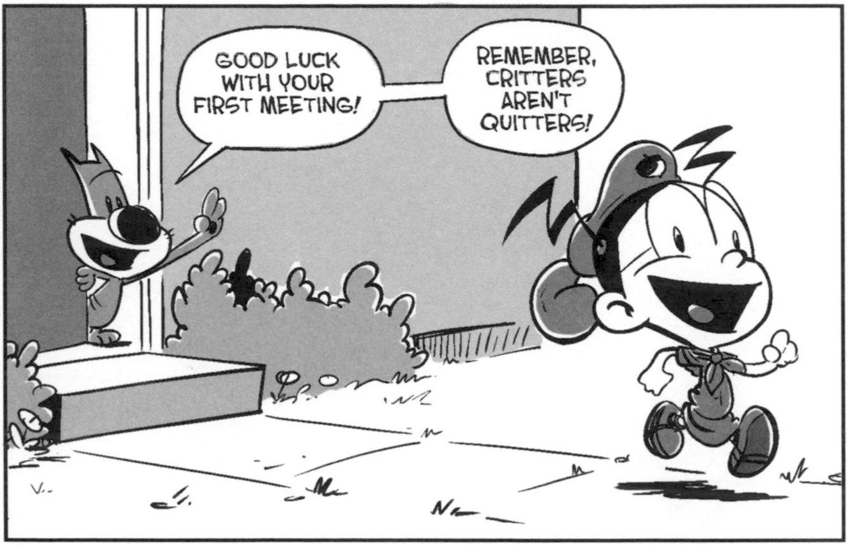
GOOD LUCK WITH YOUR FIRST MEETING!
REMEMBER, CRITTERS AREN'T QUITTERS!

A FEW HOURS LATER...

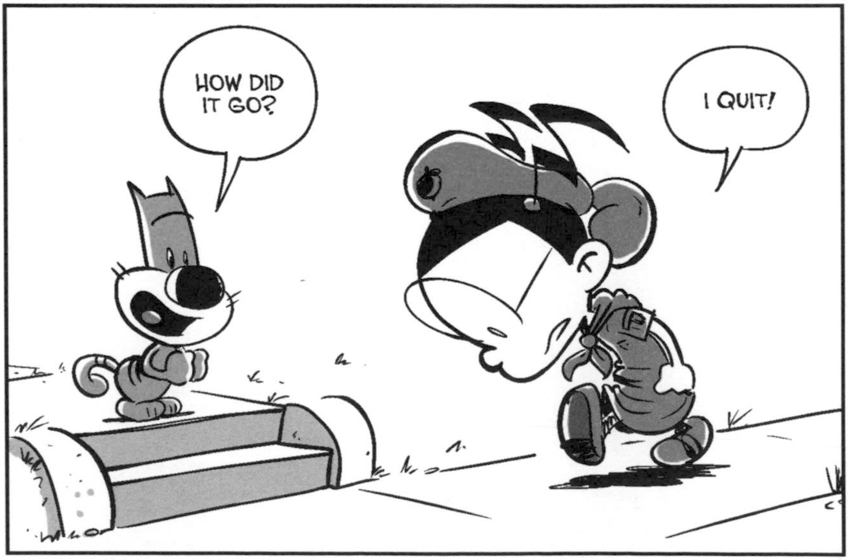
HOW DID IT GO?
I QUIT!

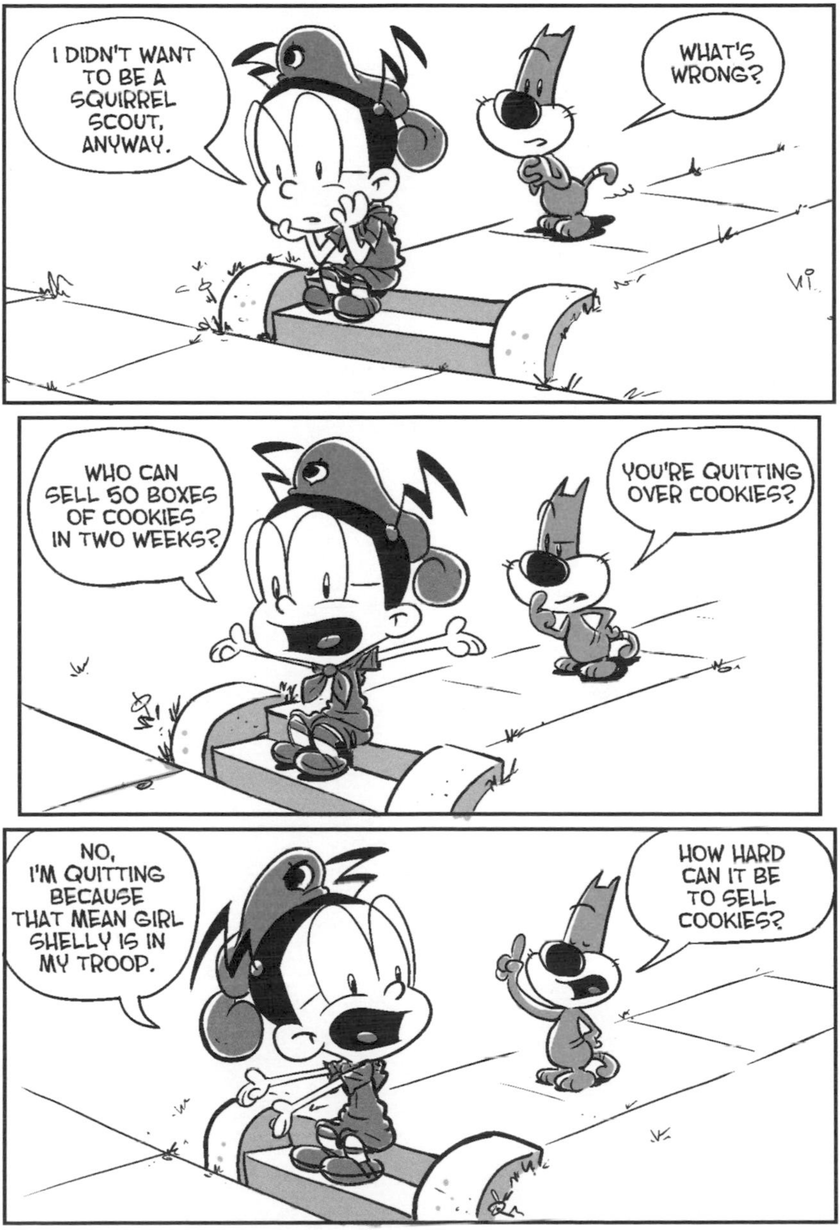
I DIDN'T WANT TO BE A SQUIRREL SCOUT, ANYWAY.
WHAT'S WRONG?
WHO CAN SELL 50 BOXES OF COOKIES IN TWO WEEKS?
YOU'RE QUITTING OVER COOKIES?
NO, I'M QUITTING BECAUSE THAT MEAN GIRL SHELLY IS IN MY TROOP.
HOW HARD CAN IT BE TO SELL COOKIES?

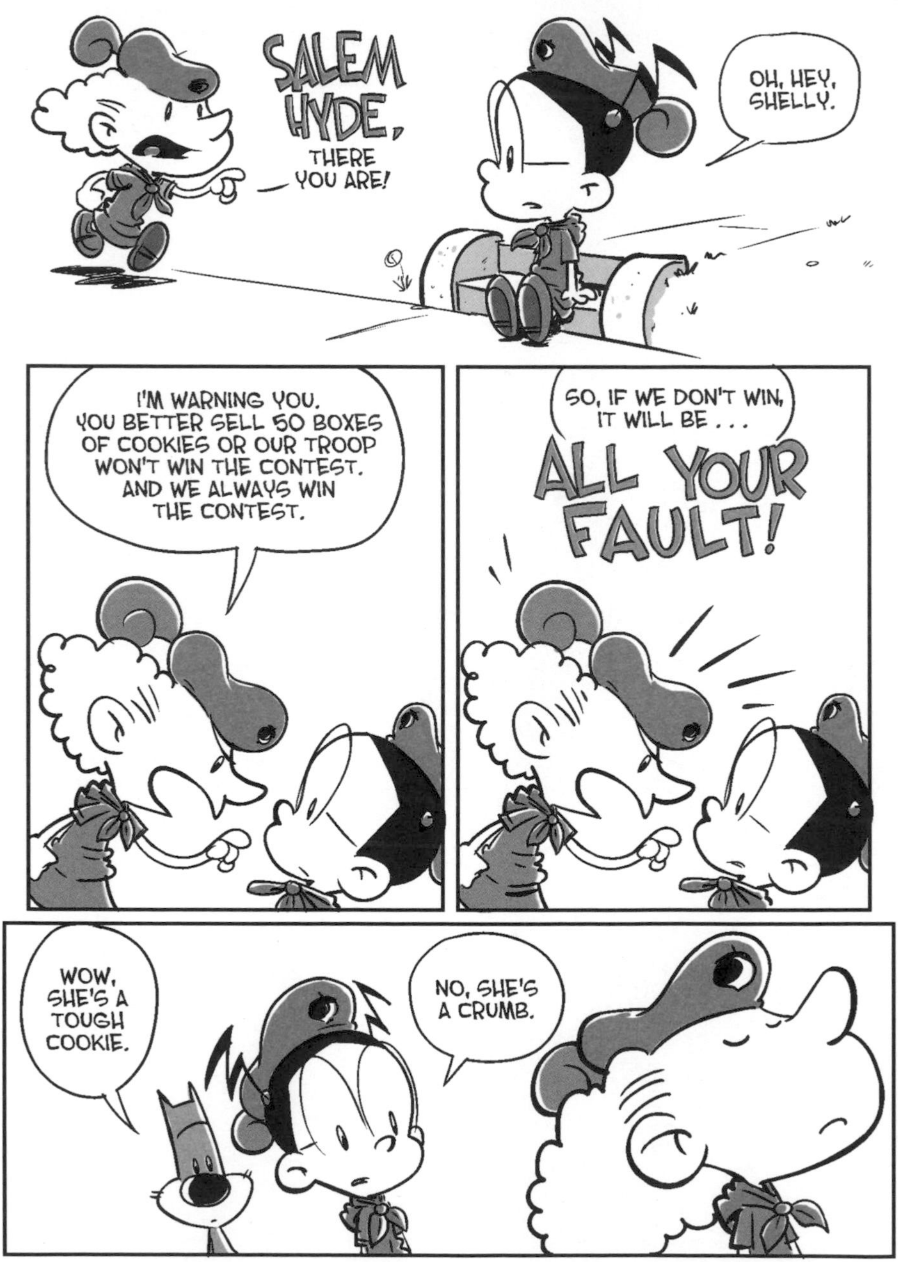
SALEM HYDE, THERE YOU ARE!
OH, HEY, SHELLY.
I'M WARNING YOU. YOU BETTER SELL 50 BOXES OF COOKIES OR OUR TROOP WON'T WIN THE CONTEST. AND WE ALWAYS WIN THE CONTEST.
SO, IF WE DON'T WIN, IT WILL BE . . .
ALL YOUR FAULT!
WOW, SHE'S A TOUGH COOKIE.
NO, SHE'S A CRUMB.

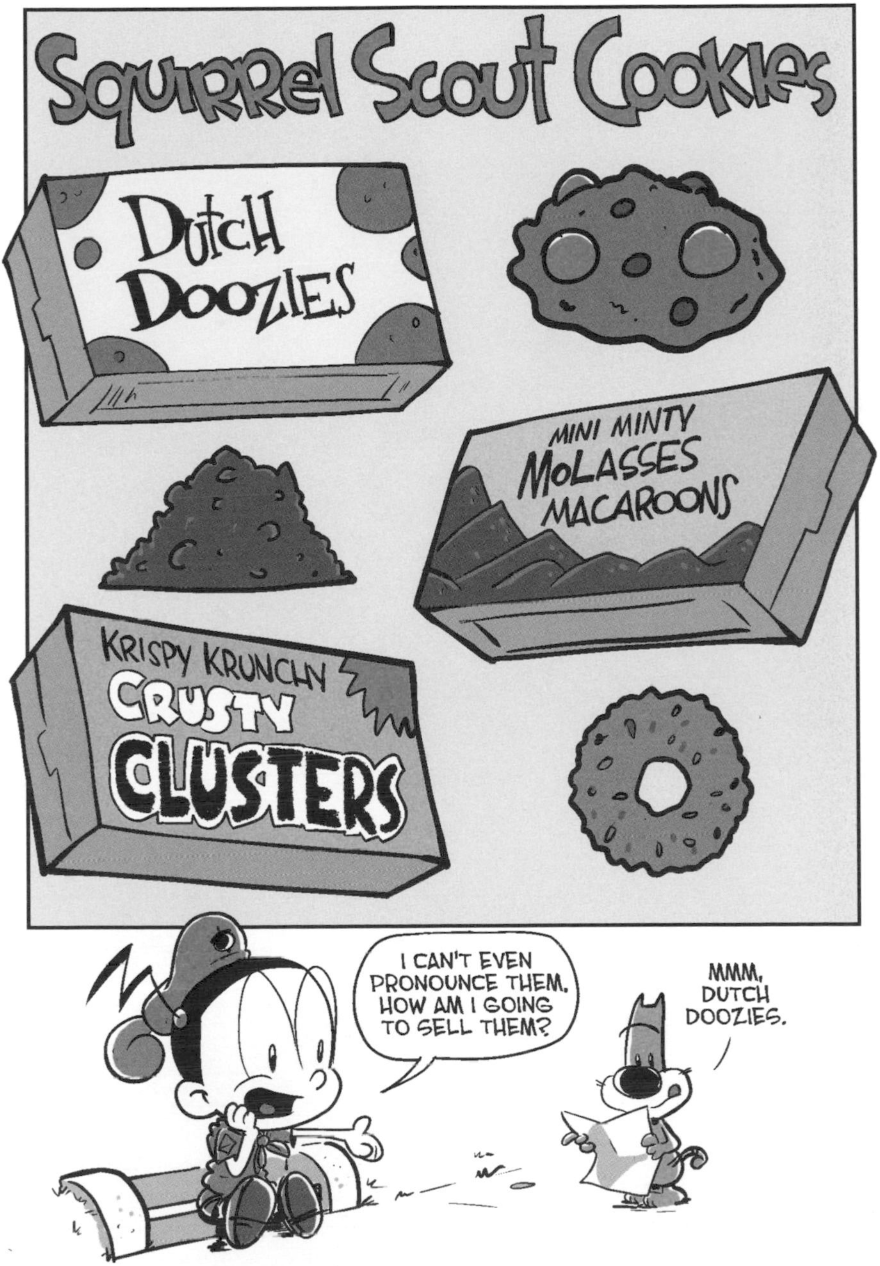
Squirrel Scout Cookies
Dutch Doozies
Mini Minty Molasses Macaroons
Krispy Krunchy Crusty Clusters
I CAN'T EVEN PRONOUNCE THEM. HOW AM I GOING TO SELL THEM?
MMM, DUTCH DOOZIES.

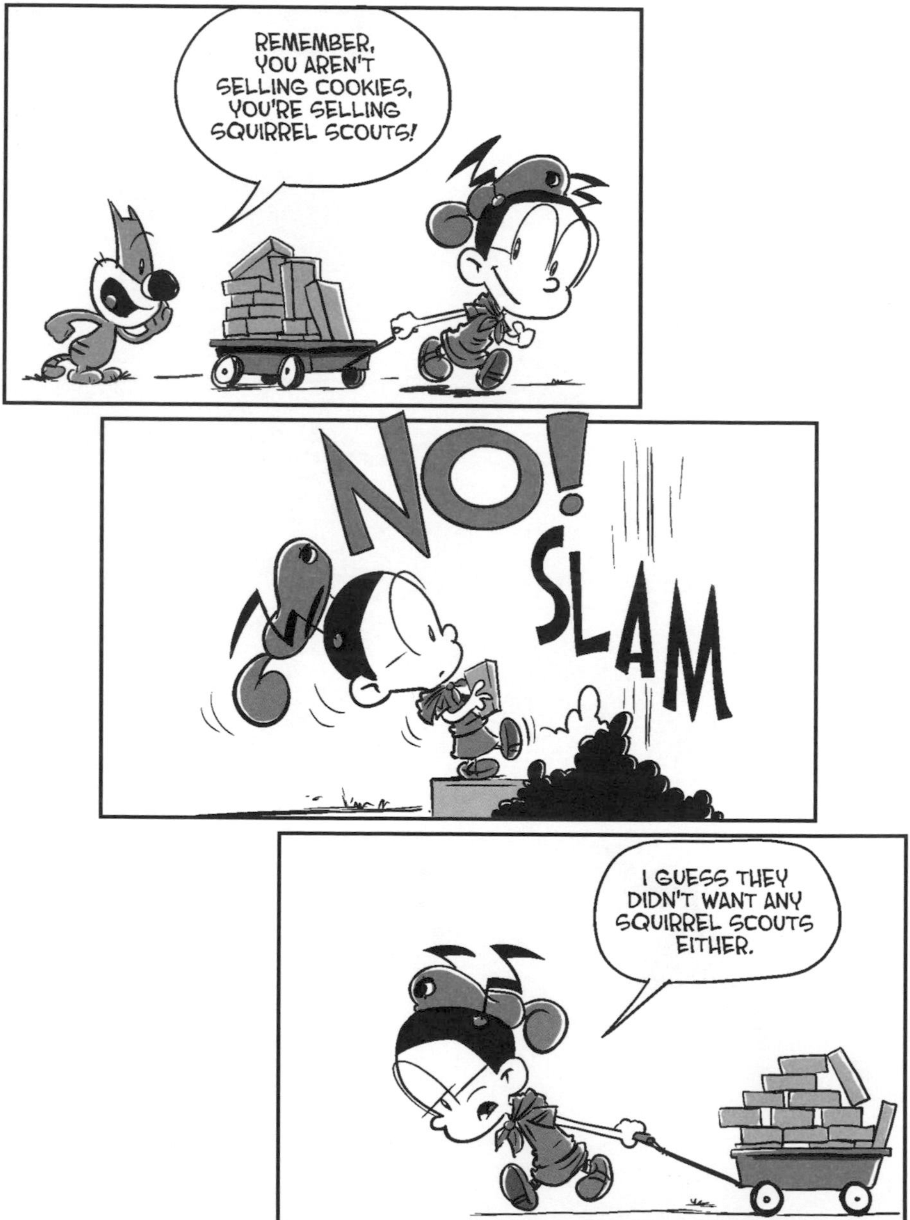
REMEMBER, YOU AREN'T SELLING COOKIES, YOU'RE SELLING SQUIRREL SCOUTS!
NO!
SLAM
I GUESS THEY DIDN'T WANT ANY SQUIRREL SCOUTS EITHER.

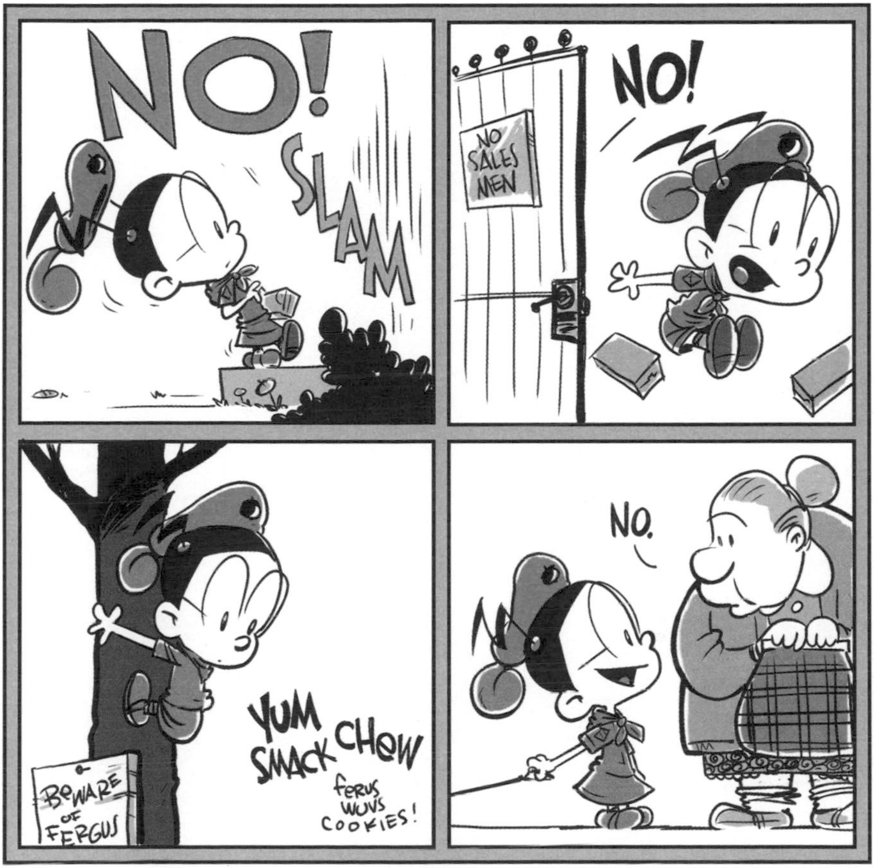

NO!
SLAM
NO SALES MEN
NO!
BEWARE OF FERGUS
YUM
SMACK
CHEW
ferus wuvs cookies!
NO.

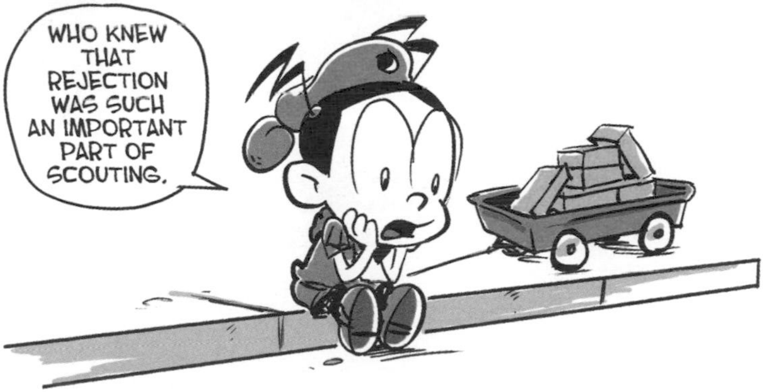

WHO KNEW THAT REJECTION WAS SUCH AN IMPORTANT PART OF SCOUTING.

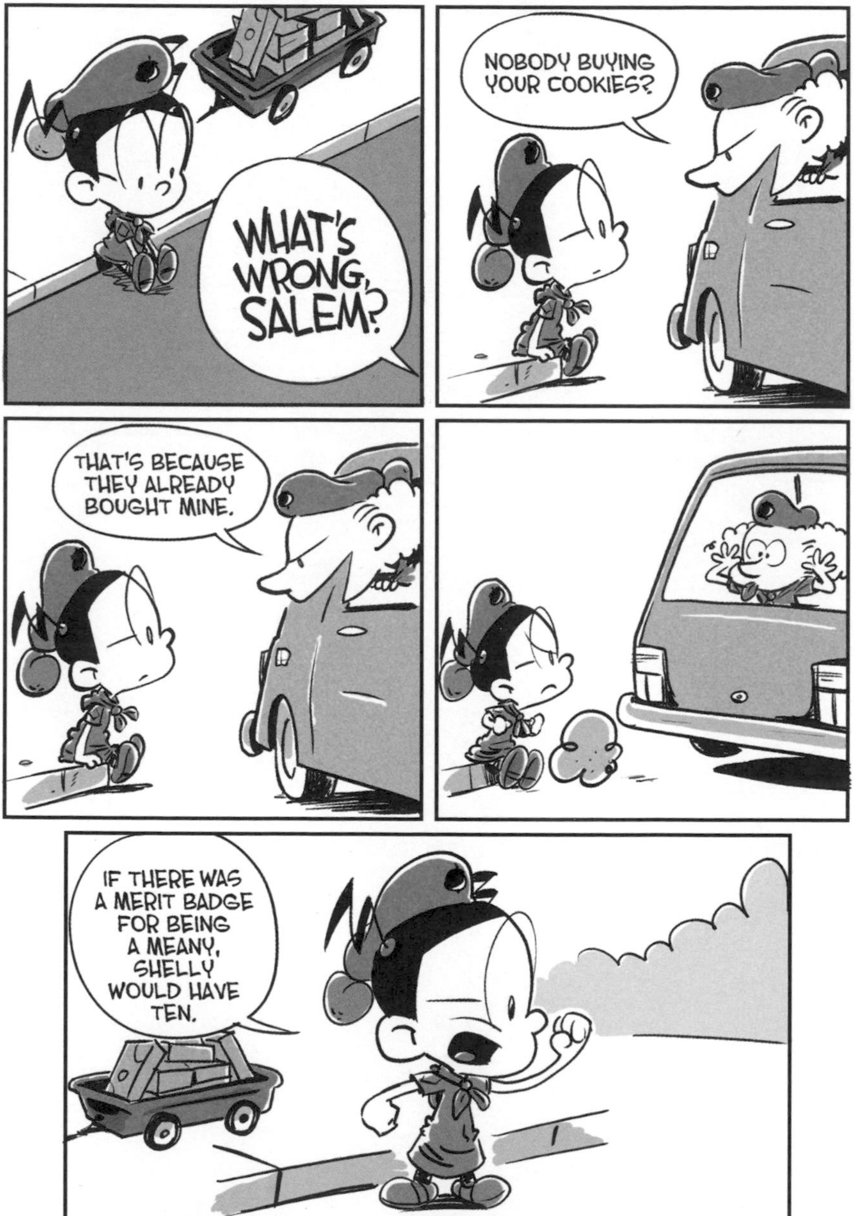
WHAT'S WRONG, SALEM?
NOBODY BUYING YOUR COOKIES?
THAT'S BECAUSE THEY ALREADY BOUGHT MINE.
IF THERE WAS A MERIT BADGE FOR BEING A MEANY, SHELLY WOULD HAVE TEN.

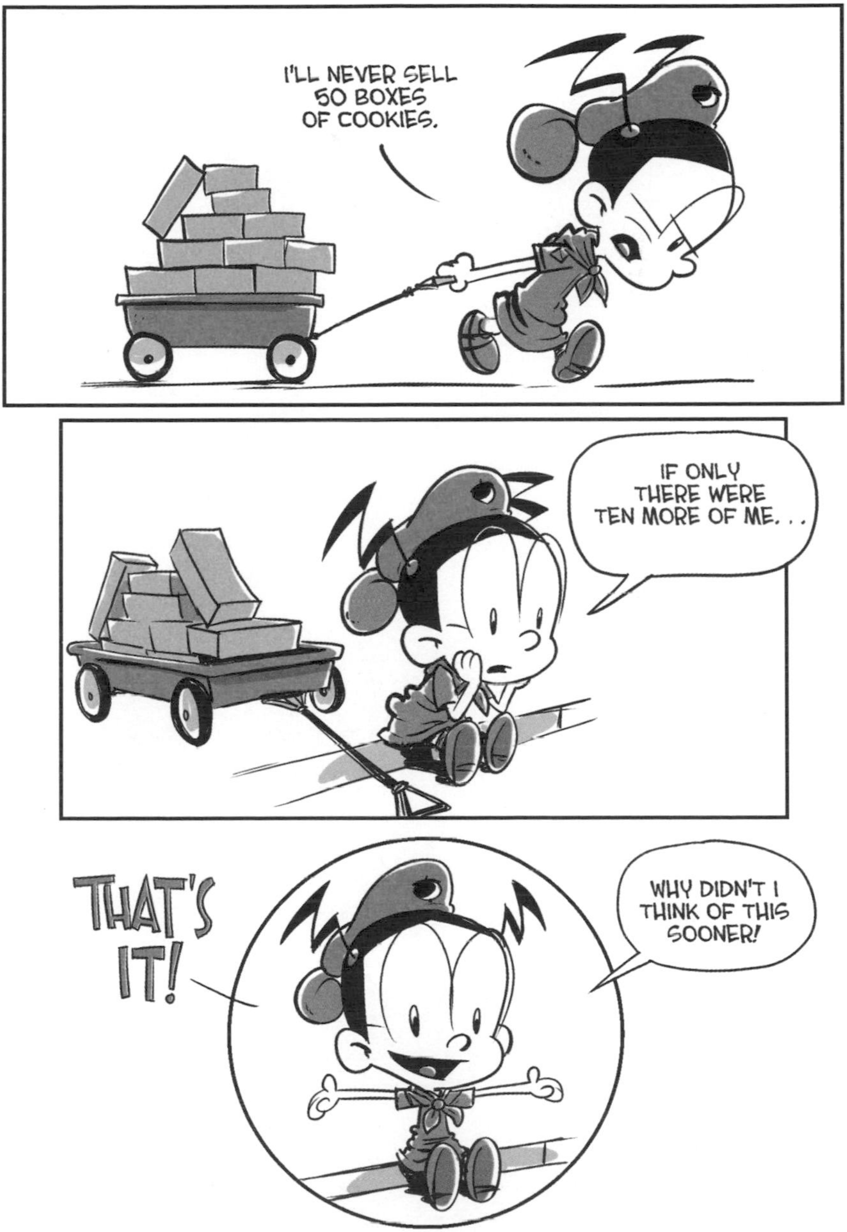

I'LL NEVER SELL 50 BOXES OF COOKIES.
IF ONLY THERE WERE TEN MORE OF ME. . .
THAT'S IT!
WHY DIDN'T I THINK OF THIS SOONER!

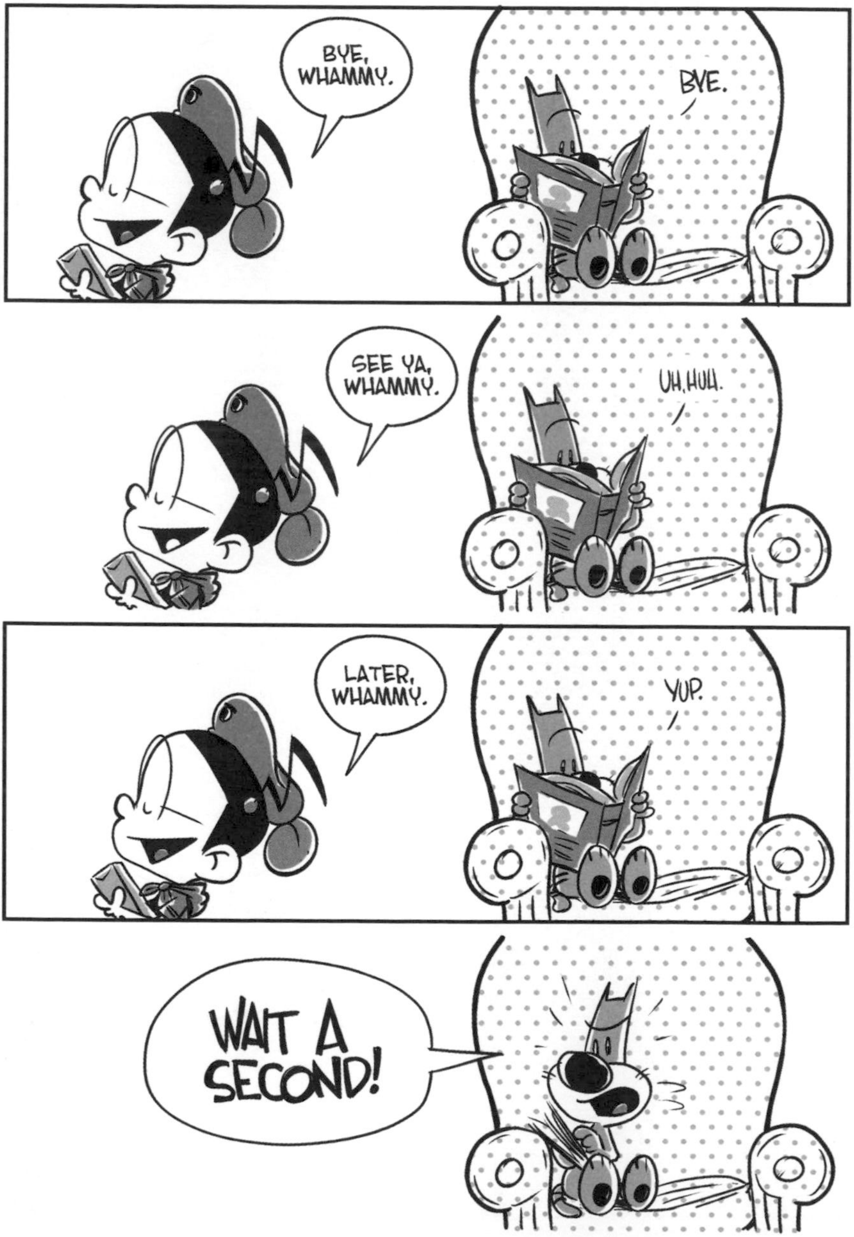
BYE, WHAMMY.
BYE.
SEE YA, WHAMMY.
UH,HUH.
LATER, WHAMMY.
YUP.
WAIT A SECOND!

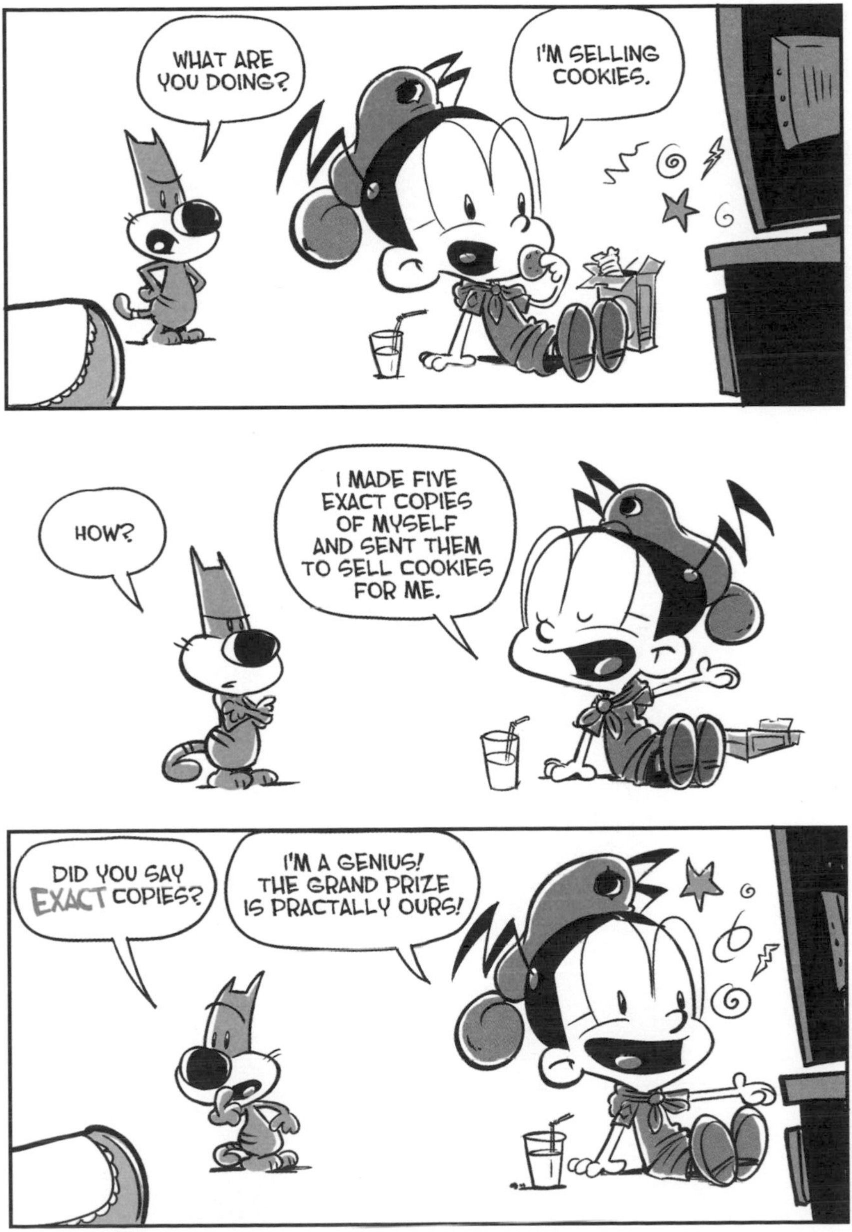
WHAT ARE YOU DOING?
I'M SELLING COOKIES.
HOW?
I MADE FIVE EXACT COPIES OF MYSELF AND SENT THEM TO SELL COOKIES FOR ME.
DID YOU SAY EXACT COPIES?
I'M A GENIUS! THE GRAND PRIZE IS PRACTALLY OURS!

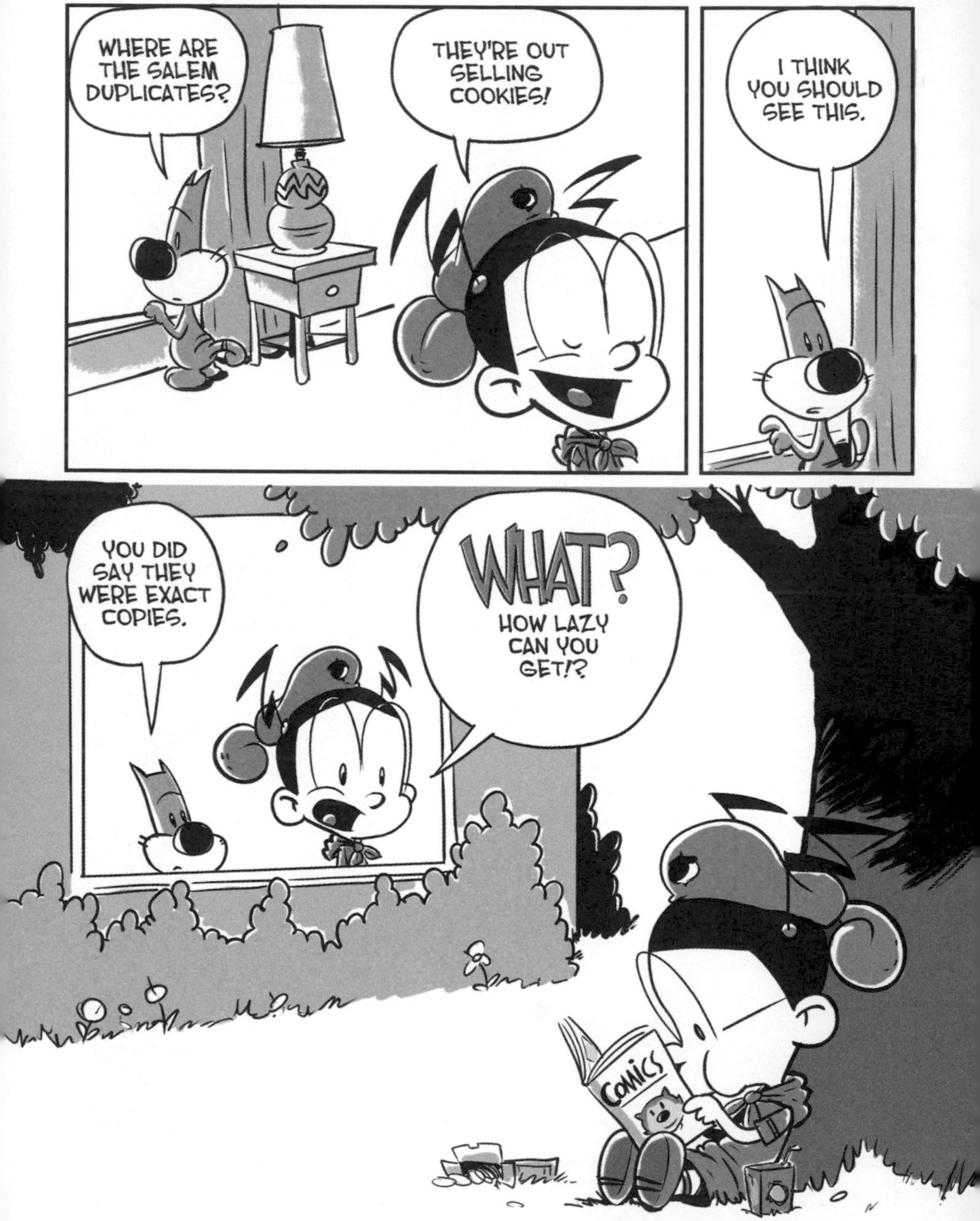
WHERE ARE THE SALEM DUPLICATES?
THEY'RE OUT SELLING COOKIES!
I THINK YOU SHOULD SEE THIS.
YOU DID SAY THEY WERE EXACT COPIES.
WHAT? HOW LAZY CAN YOU GET!?
COMICS

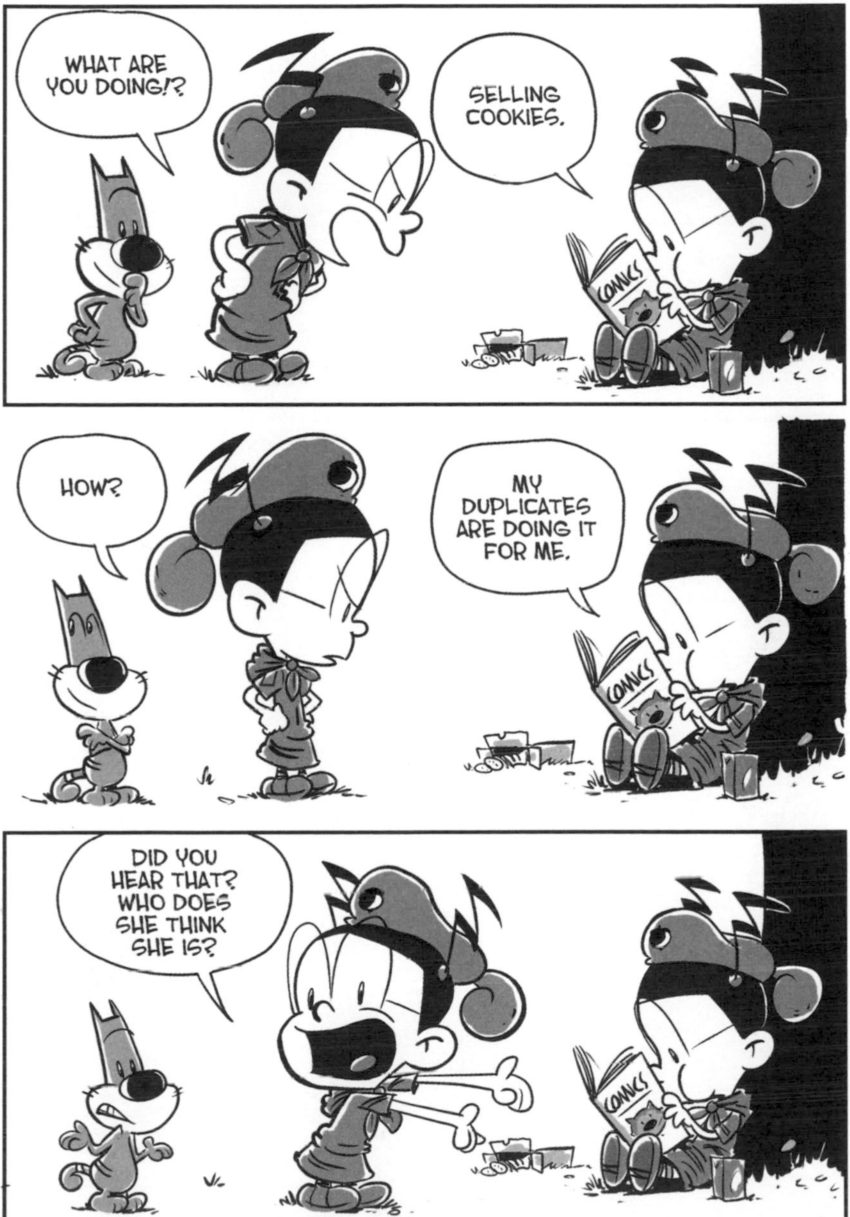
WHAT ARE YOU DOING!?
SELLING COOKIES.
COMICS
HOW?
MY DUPLICATES ARE DOING IT FOR ME.
COMICS
DID YOU HEAR THAT? WHO DOES SHE THINK SHE IS?
COMICS

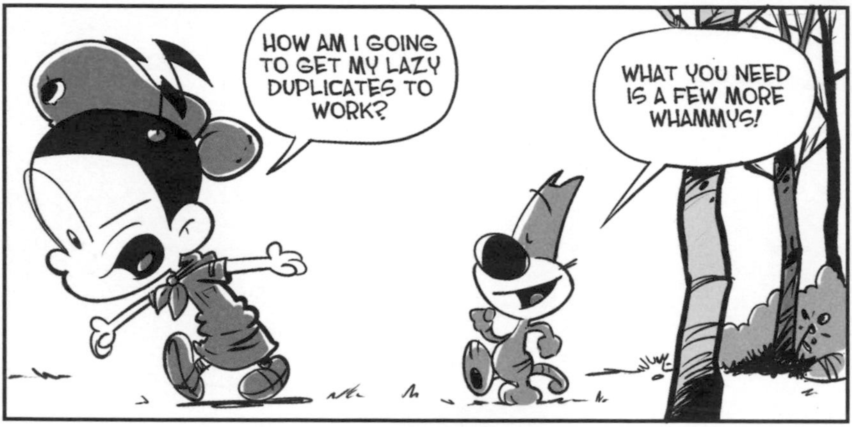
HOW AM I GOING TO GET MY LAZY DUPLICATES TO WORK?
WHAT YOU NEED IS A FEW MORE WHAMMYS!

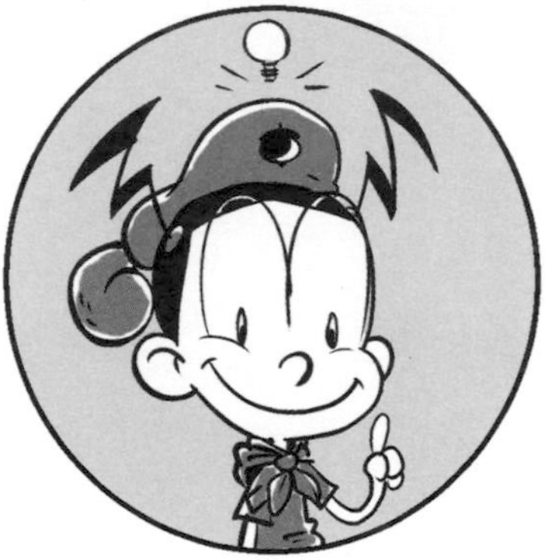

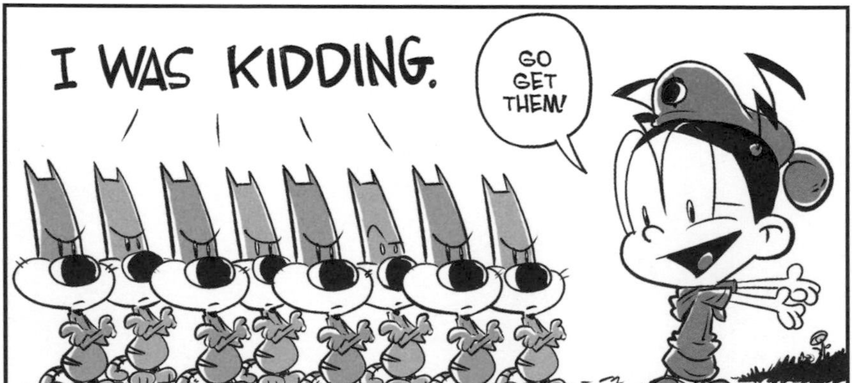
I WAS KIDDING.
GO GET THEM!

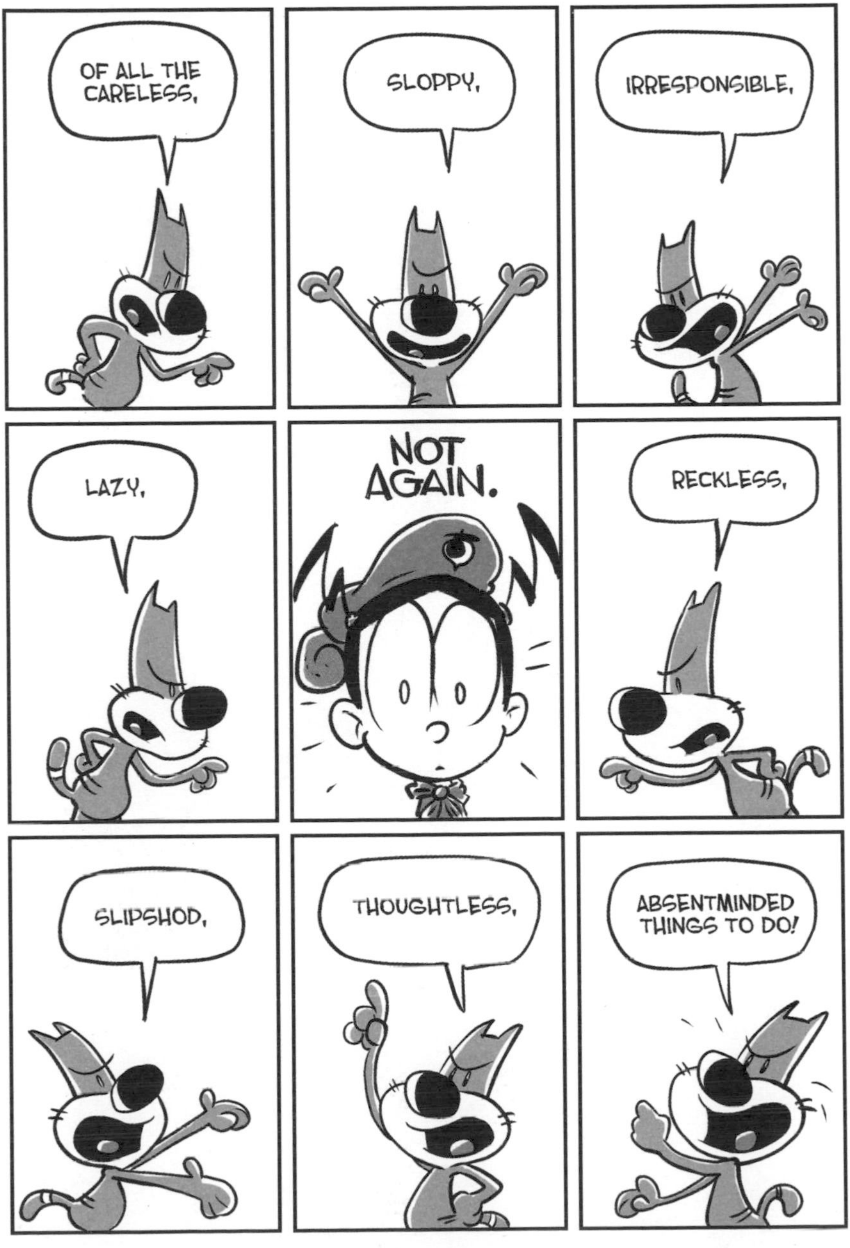

OF ALL THE CARELESS,
SLOPPY,
IRRESPONSIBLE,
LAZY,
NOT AGAIN.
RECKLESS,
SLIPSHOD,
THOUGHTLESS,
ABSENTMINDED THINGS TO DO!

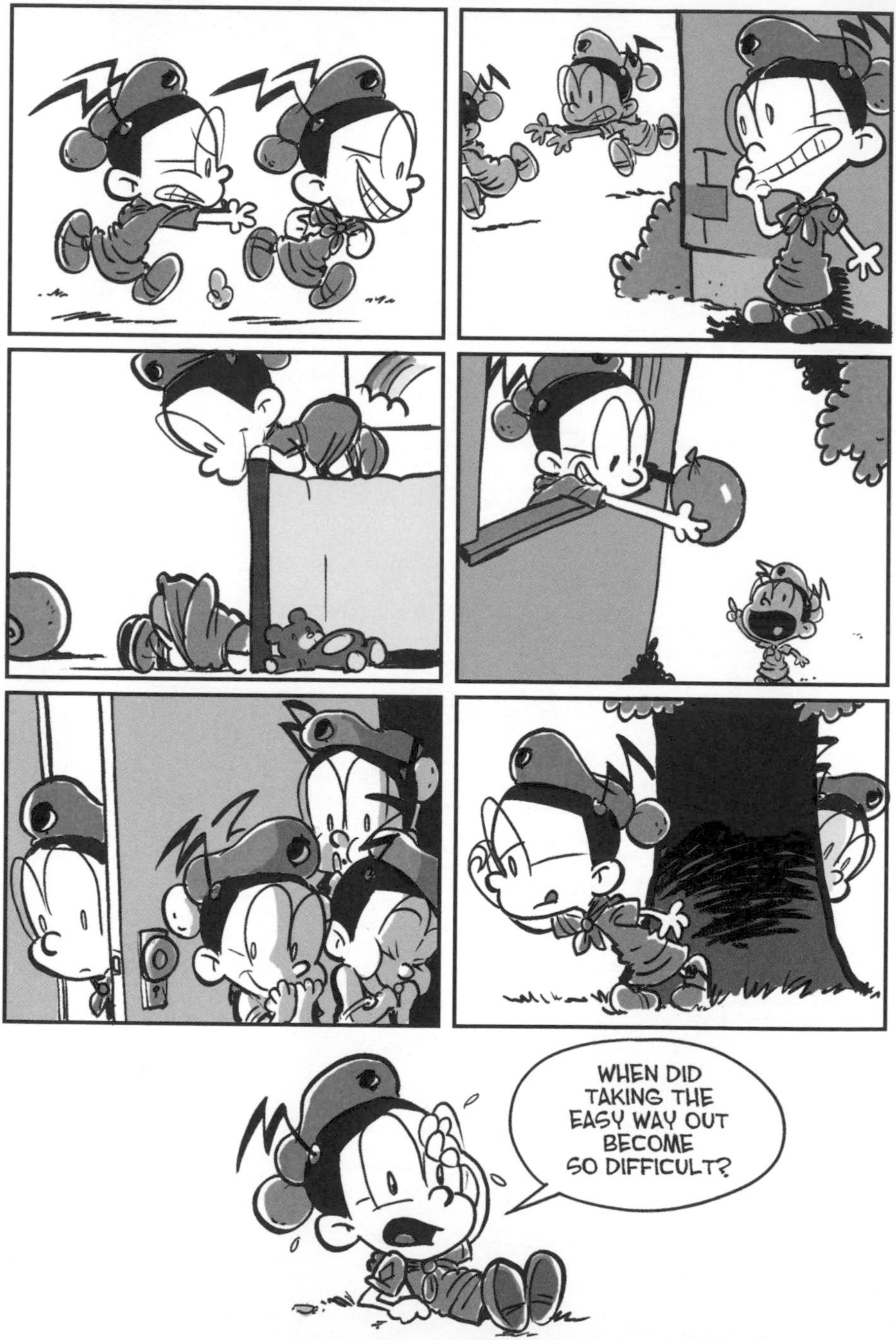
WHEN DID TAKING THE EASY WAY OUT BECOME SO DIFFICULT?

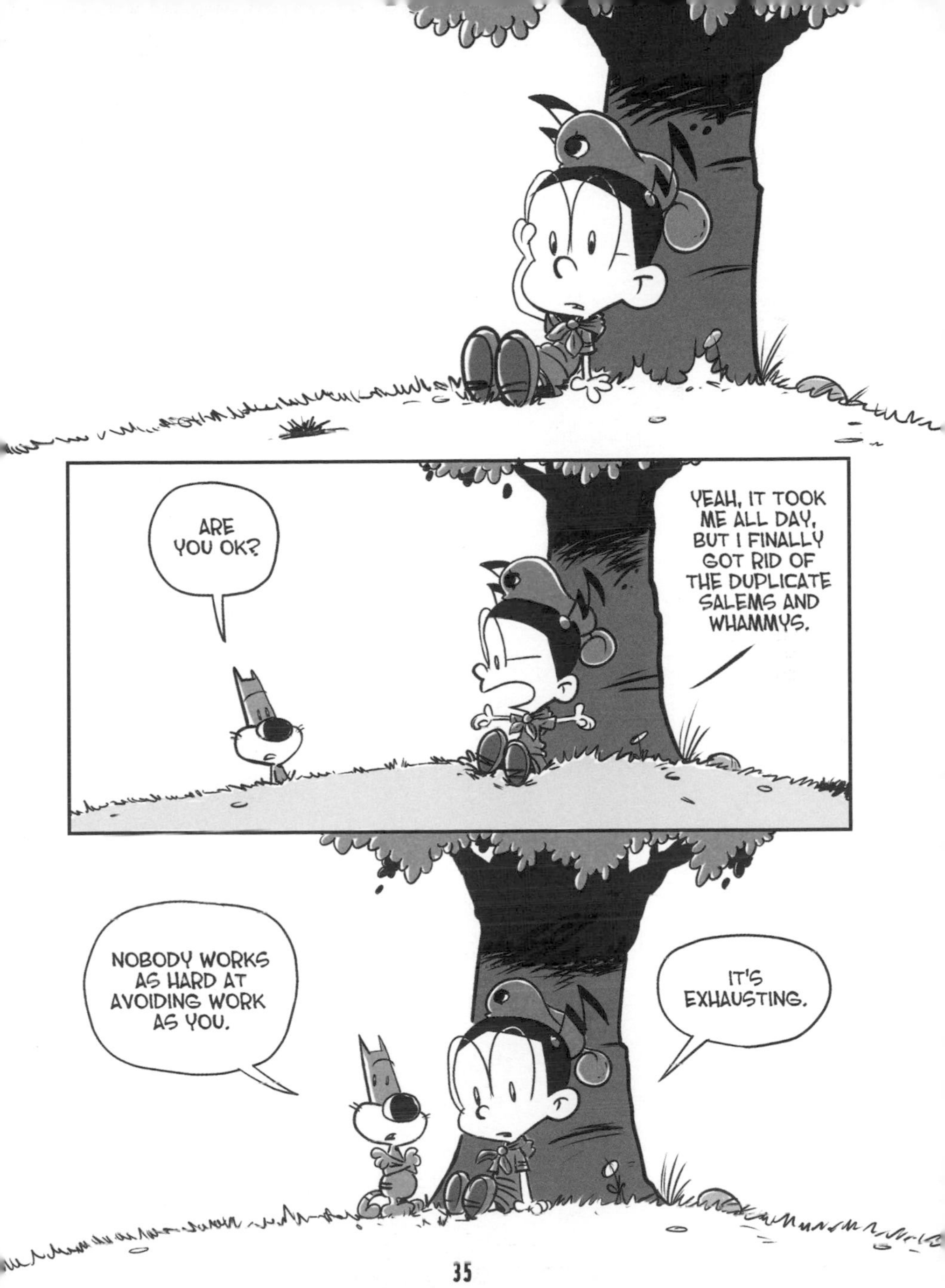
ARE YOU OK?
YEAH, IT TOOK ME ALL DAY, BUT I FINALLY GOT RID OF THE DUPLICATE SALEMS AND WHAMMYS.
NOBODY WORKS AS HARD AT AVOIDING WORK AS YOU.
IT'S EXHAUSTING.

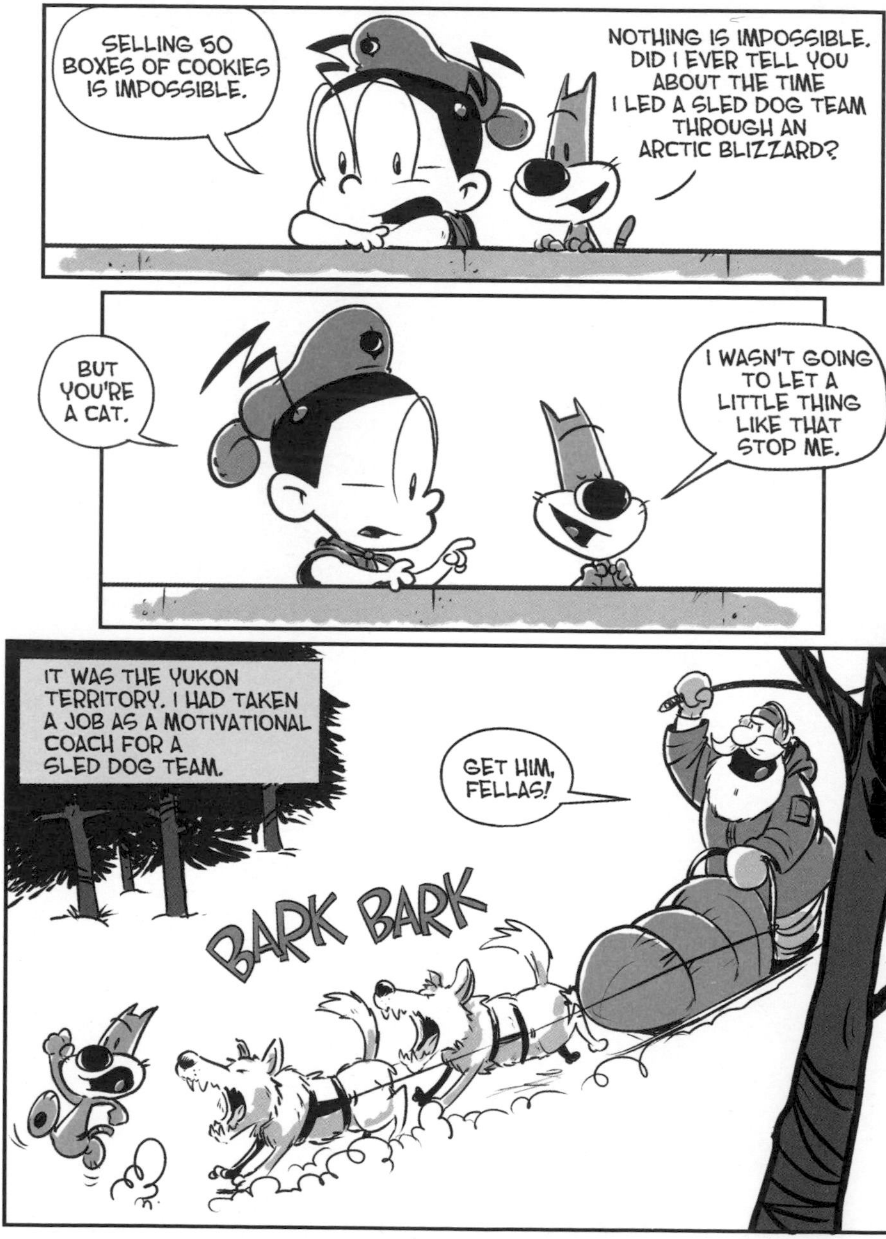
SELLING 50 BOXES OF COOKIES IS IMPOSSIBLE.
NOTHING IS IMPOSSIBLE. DID I EVER TELL YOU ABOUT THE TIME I LED A SLED DOG TEAM THROUGH AN ARCTIC BLIZZARD?
BUT YOU'RE A CAT.
I WASN'T GOING TO LET A LITTLE THING LIKE THAT STOP ME.
IT WAS THE YUKON TERRITORY. I HAD TAKEN A JOB AS A MOTIVATIONAL COACH FOR A SLED DOG TEAM.
GET HIM, FELLAS!
BARK BARK

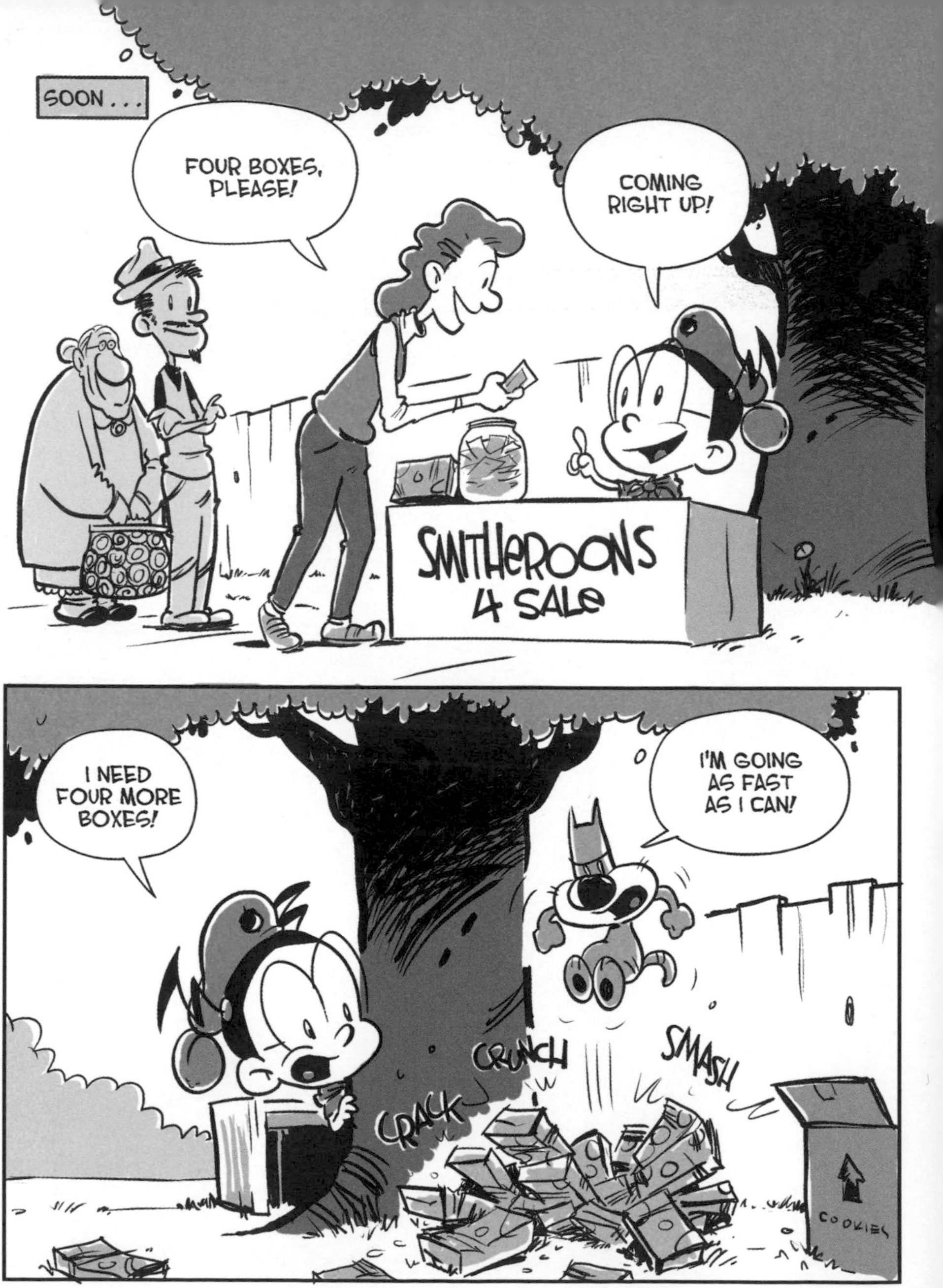
SOON . . .
FOUR BOXES, PLEASE!
COMING RIGHT UP!
SMITHEROONS 4 SALE
I NEED FOUR MORE BOXES!
I'M GOING AS FAST AS I CAN!
CRUNCH
SMASH
CRACK
COOKIES

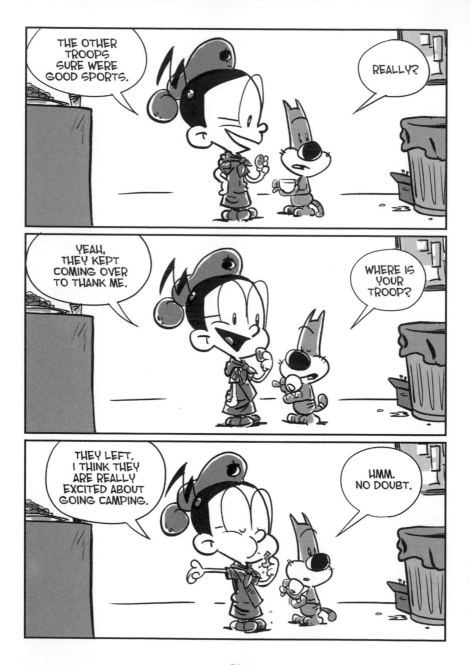

PART 2
Squirrel Scout GUIDE TO CAMPING

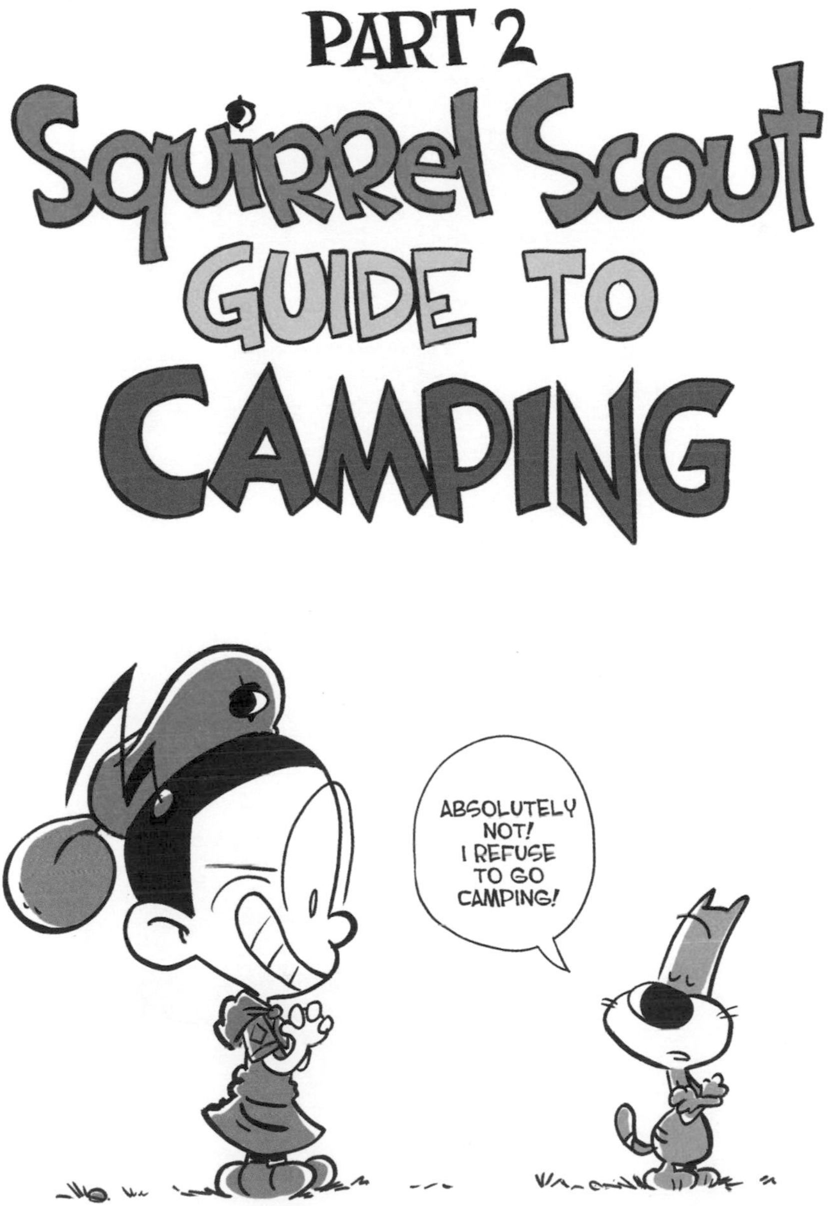
ABSOLUTELY NOT! I REFUSE TO GO CAMPING!

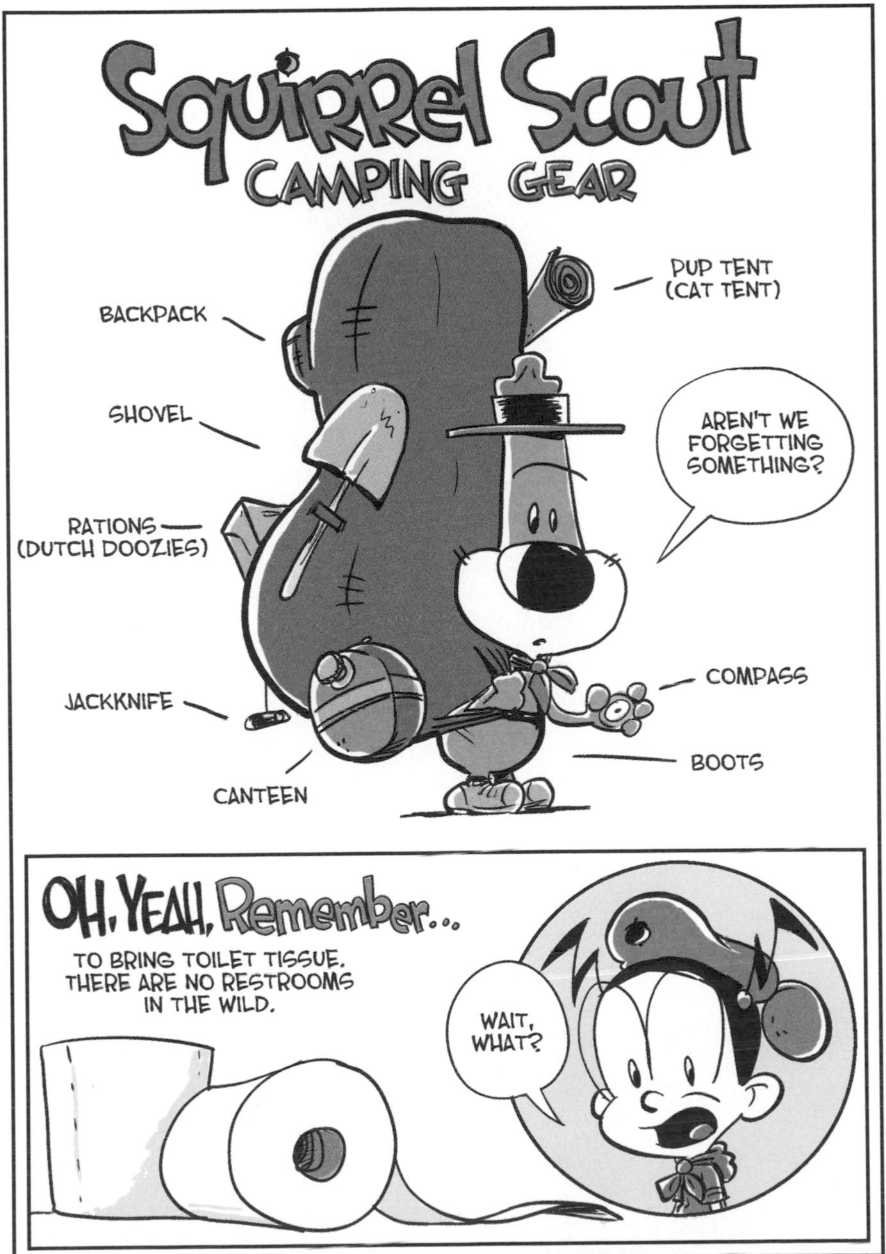
Squirrel Scout
CAMPING GEAR
PUP TENT (CAT TENT)
BACKPACK
SHOVEL
AREN'T WE FORGETTING SOMETHING?
RATIONS (DUTCH DOOZIES)
COMPASS
JACKKNIFE
BOOTS
CANTEEN
OH, YEAH, Remember...
TO BRING TOILET TISSUE. THERE ARE NO RESTROOMS IN THE WILD.
WAIT, WHAT?

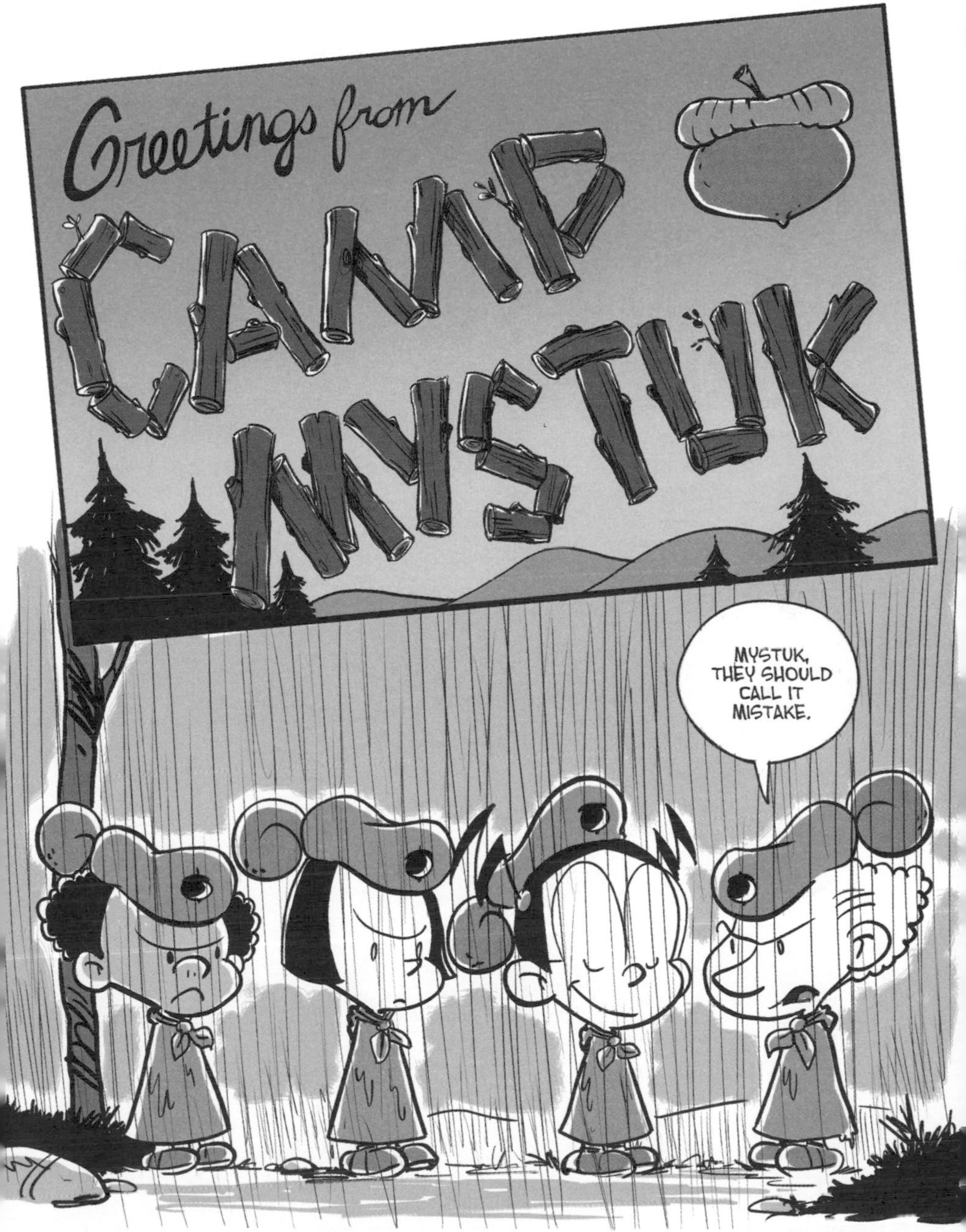
Greetings from
CAMP
MYSTUK
MYSTUK, THEY SHOULD CALL IT MISTAKE.

Getting to Know... MR. FINK

TEACHER, STORE MANAGER, SCOUTMASTER,
AND LITTLE LEAGUE UMPIRE

LIKES

ORDER
QUIET
PEACE

DISLIKES

FUN (IN GENERAL)
PUPPIES
GUPPIES
BIKES
TRIKES
TYKES
CANDY
TOYS
PARTIES
VIDEO GAMES
PIZZA
CARTOONS
BALLOONS
MACAROONS
BASSOONS
LEGUMES
CATS
CHAOS
KIDS
(ALL KINDS, BUT
ESPECIALLY SALEM HYDE)

DID YOU KNOW...

MR. FINK CANNOT SEE
WITHOUT HIS
GLASSES.

63

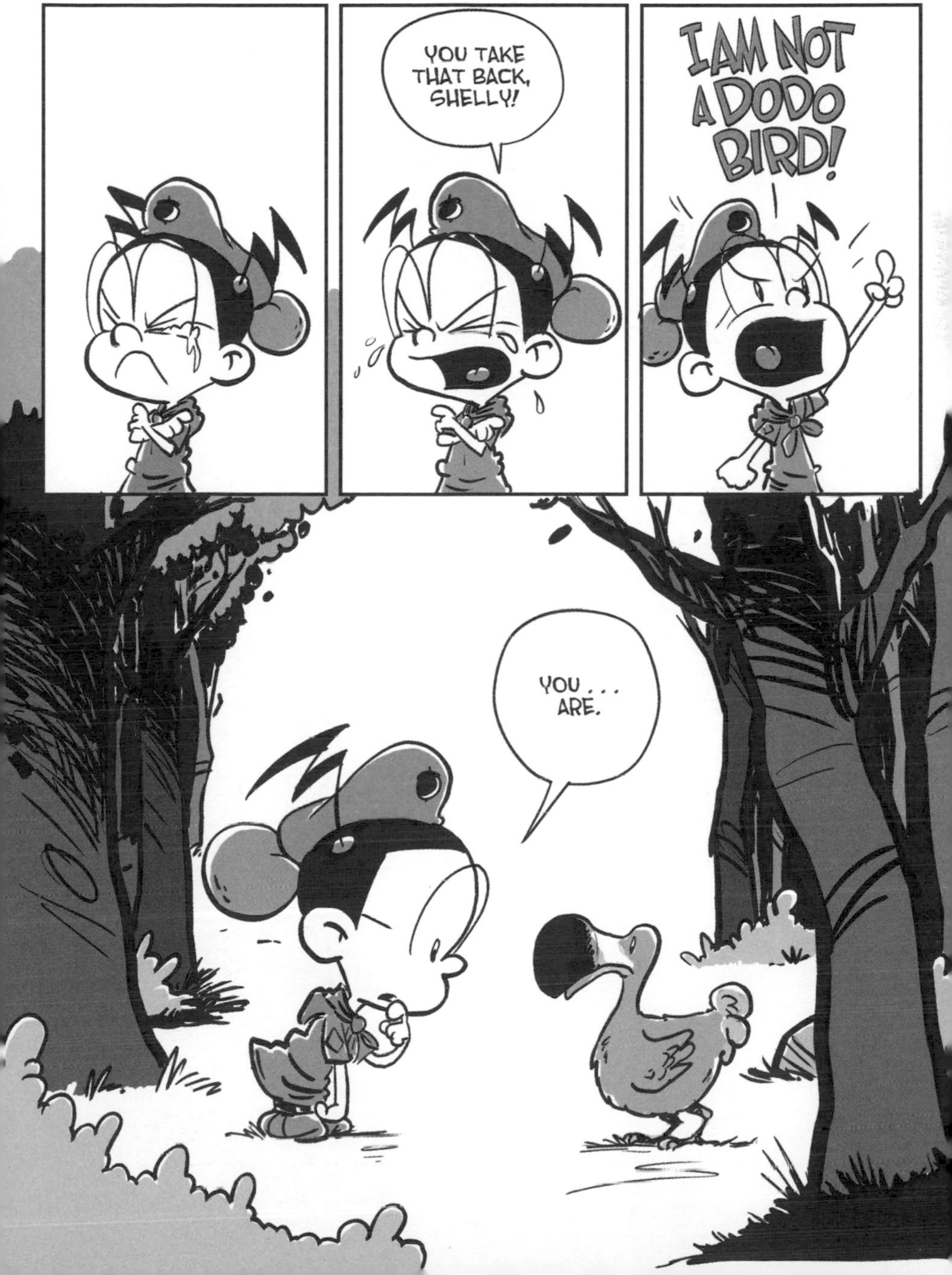
YOU TAKE THAT BACK, SHELLY!
I AM NOT A DODO BIRD!
YOU . . . ARE.

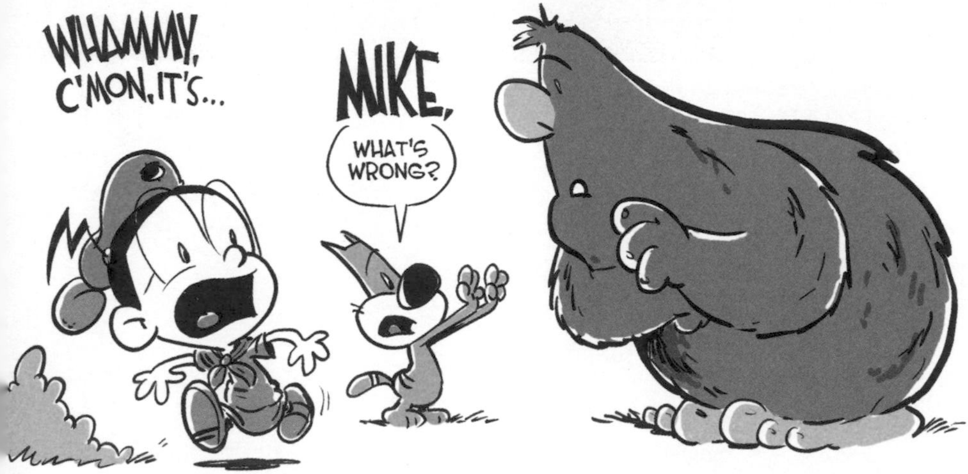
WHAMMY,
C'MON, IT'S...
MIKE,
WHAT'S WRONG?

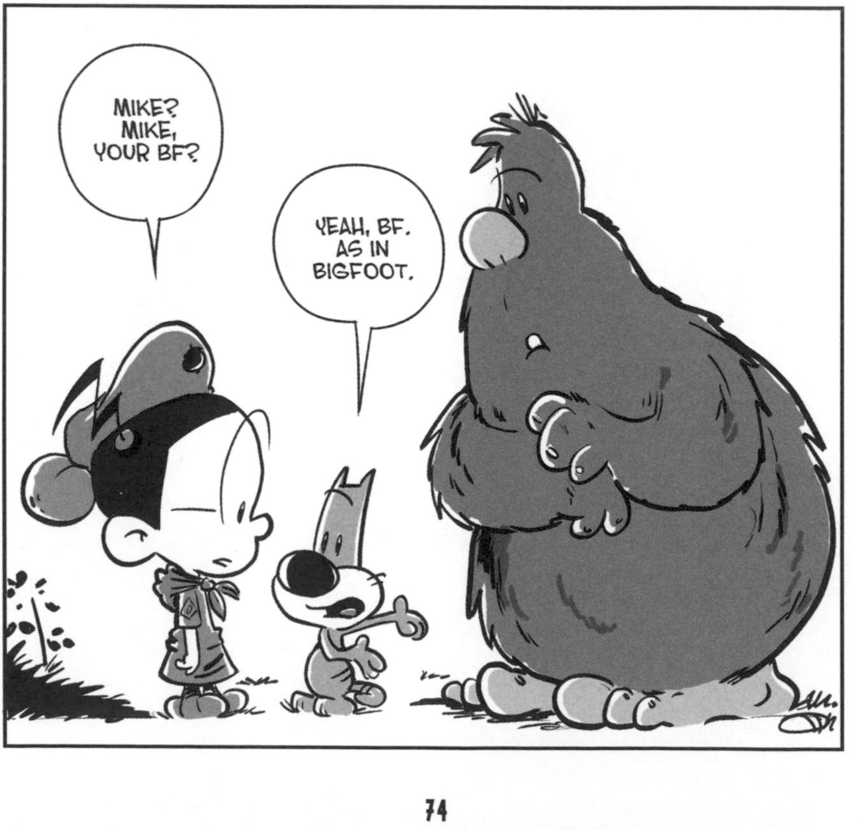
MIKE? MIKE, YOUR BF?
YEAH, BF. AS IN BIGFOOT.

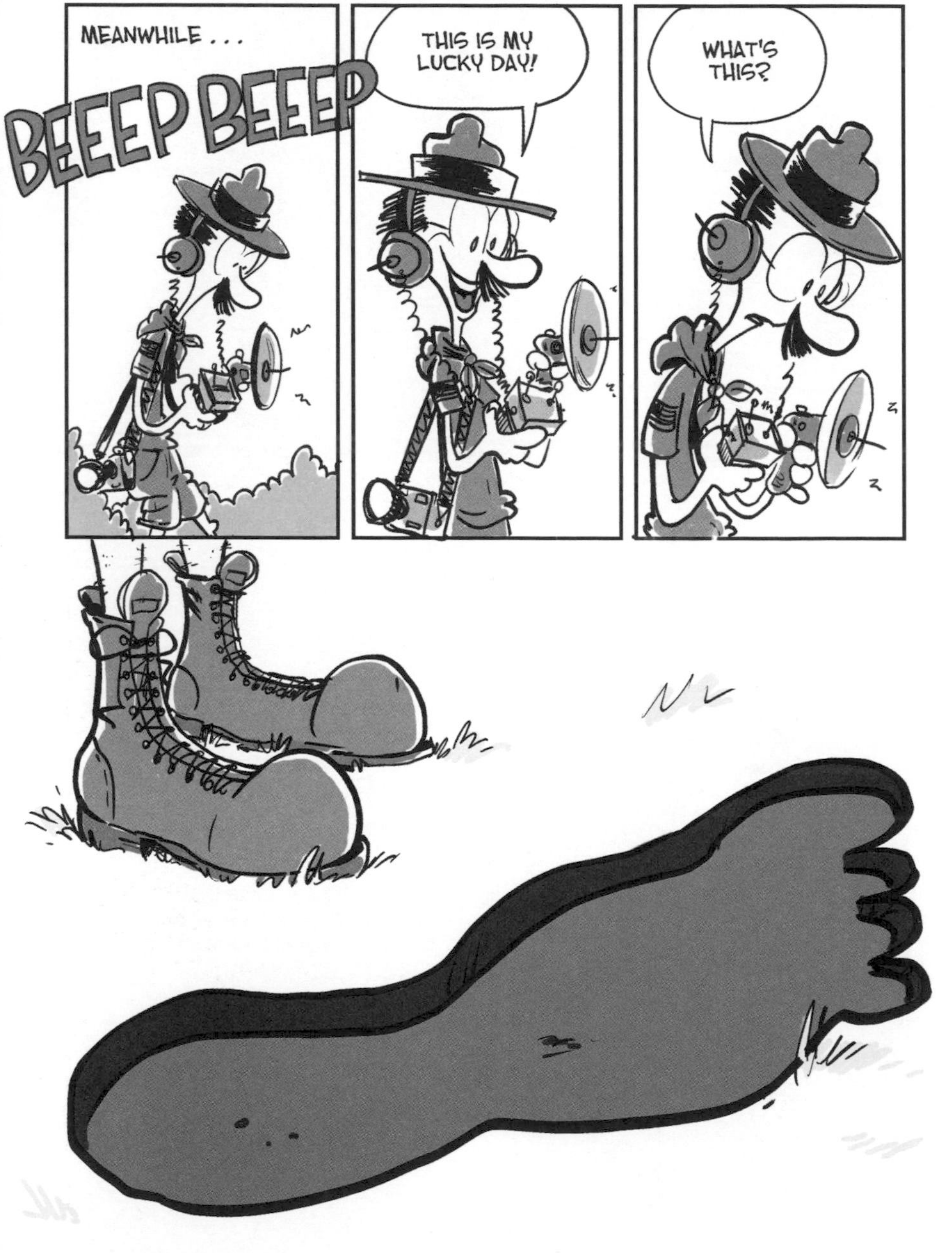
MEANWHILE . . .
BEEEP BEEEP
THIS IS MY LUCKY DAY!
WHAT'S THIS?

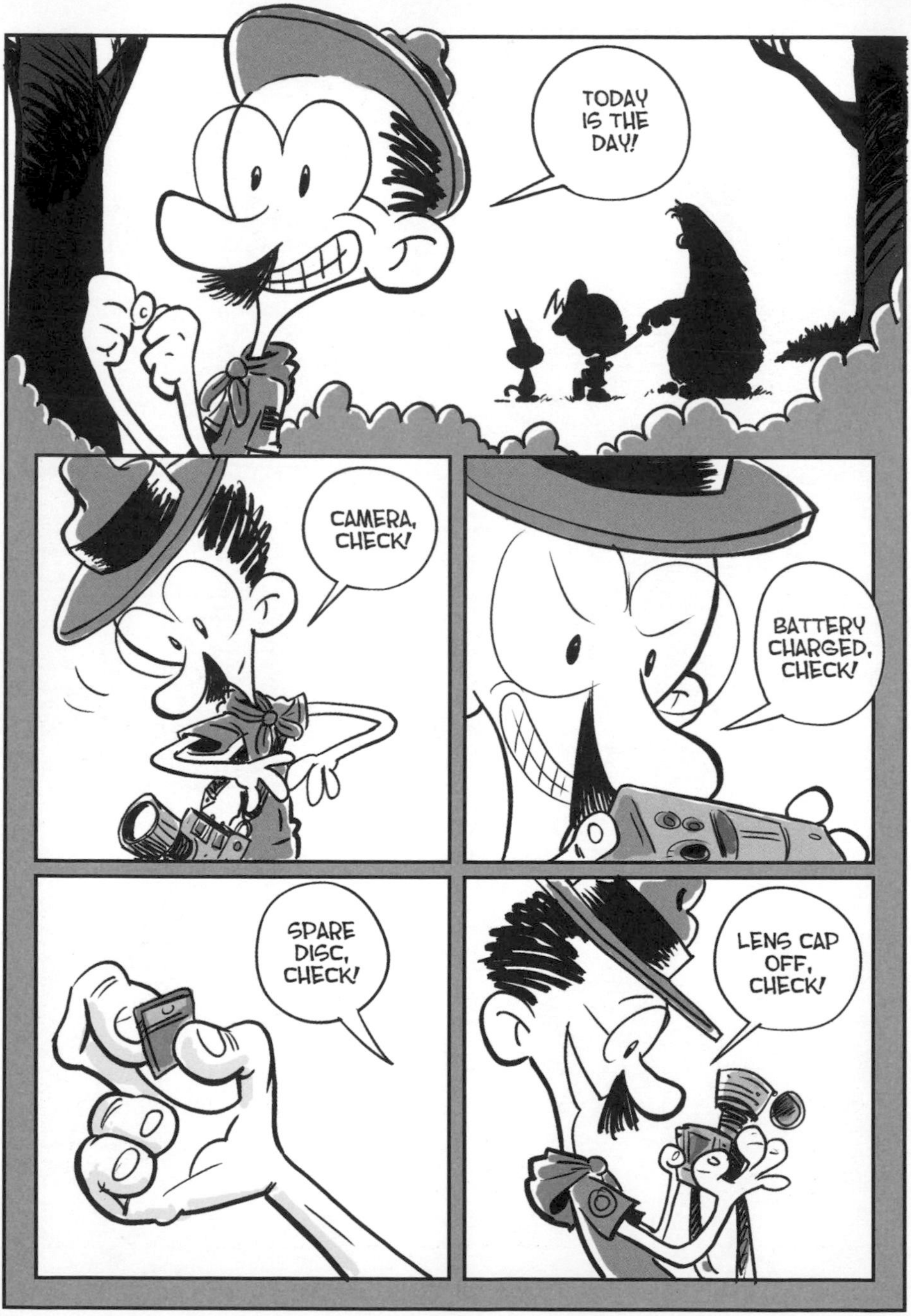
TODAY IS THE DAY!
CAMERA, CHECK!
BATTERY CHARGED, CHECK!
SPARE DISC, CHECK!
LENS CAP OFF, CHECK!

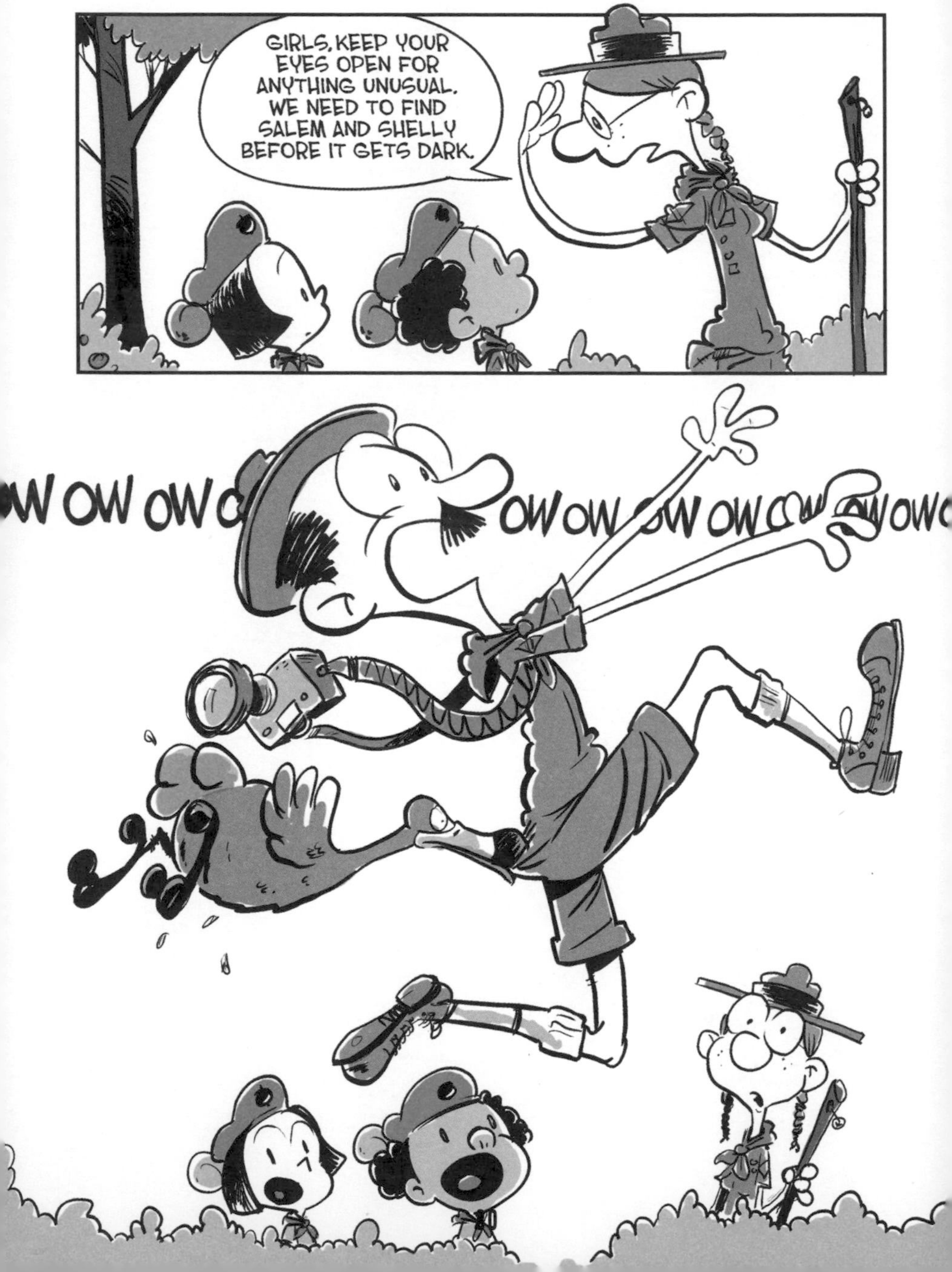
GIRLS, KEEP YOUR EYES OPEN FOR ANYTHING UNUSUAL. WE NEED TO FIND SALEM AND SHELLY BEFORE IT GETS DARK.
OW OW OW OW OW OW OW OW OW OW

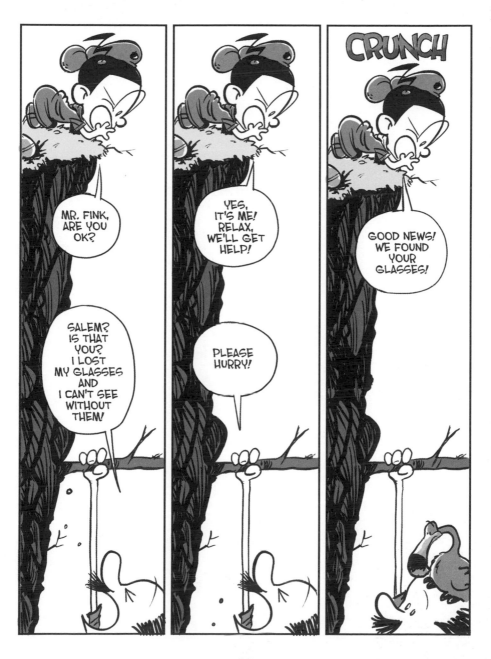

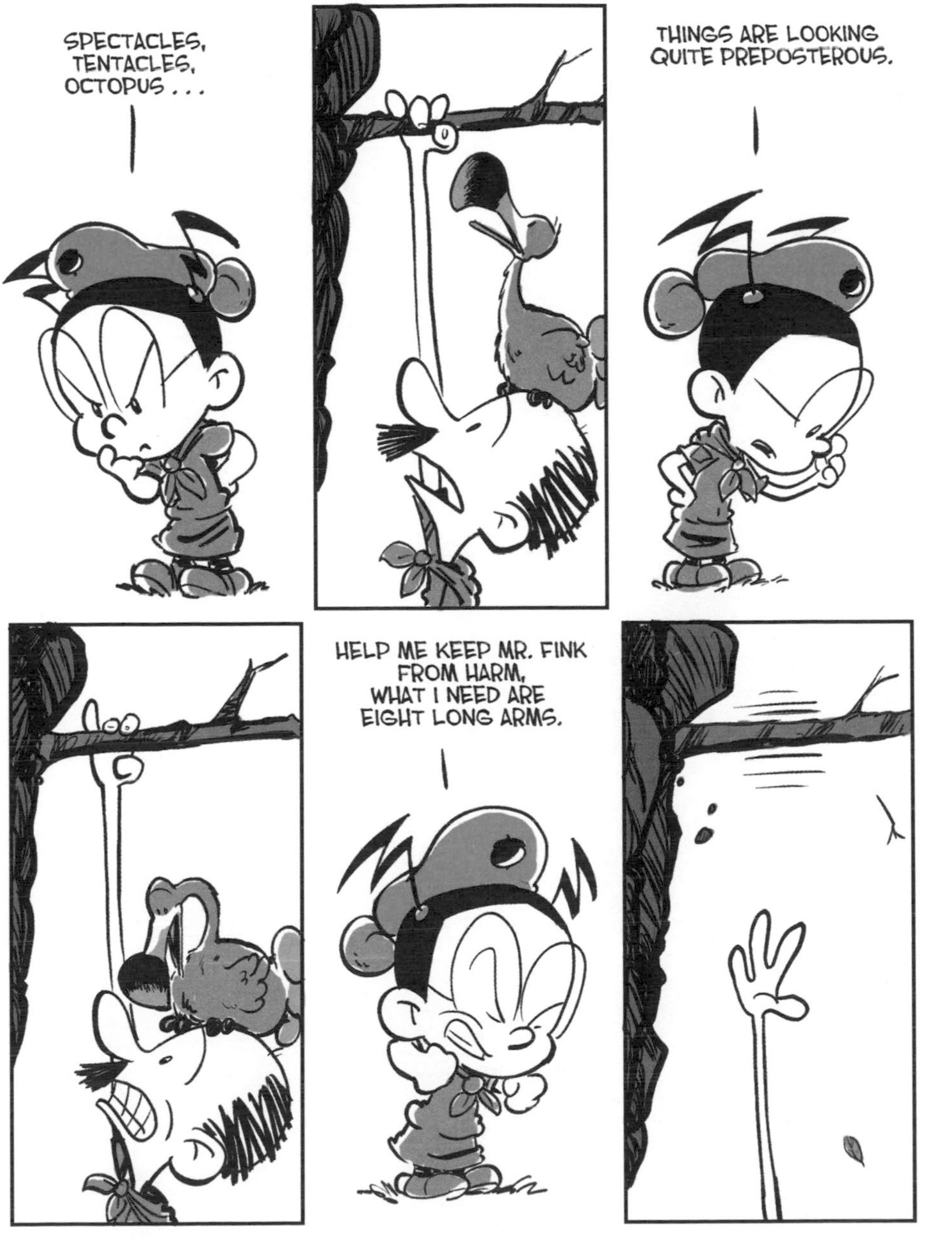
SPECTACLES, TENTACLES, OCTOPUS . . .
THINGS ARE LOOKING QUITE PREPOSTEROUS.
HELP ME KEEP MR. FINK FROM HARM, WHAT I NEED ARE EIGHT LONG ARMS.

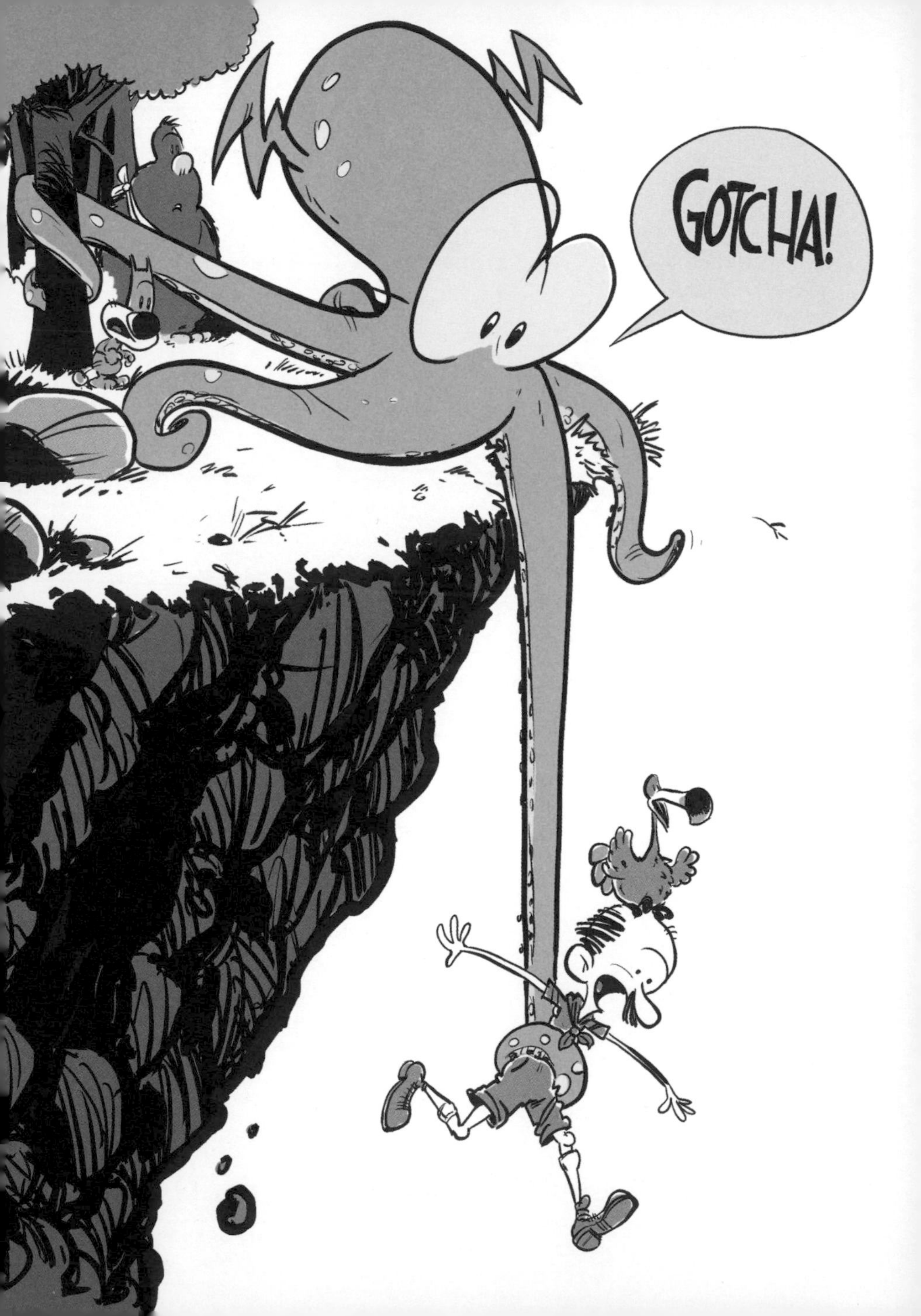
GOTCHA!

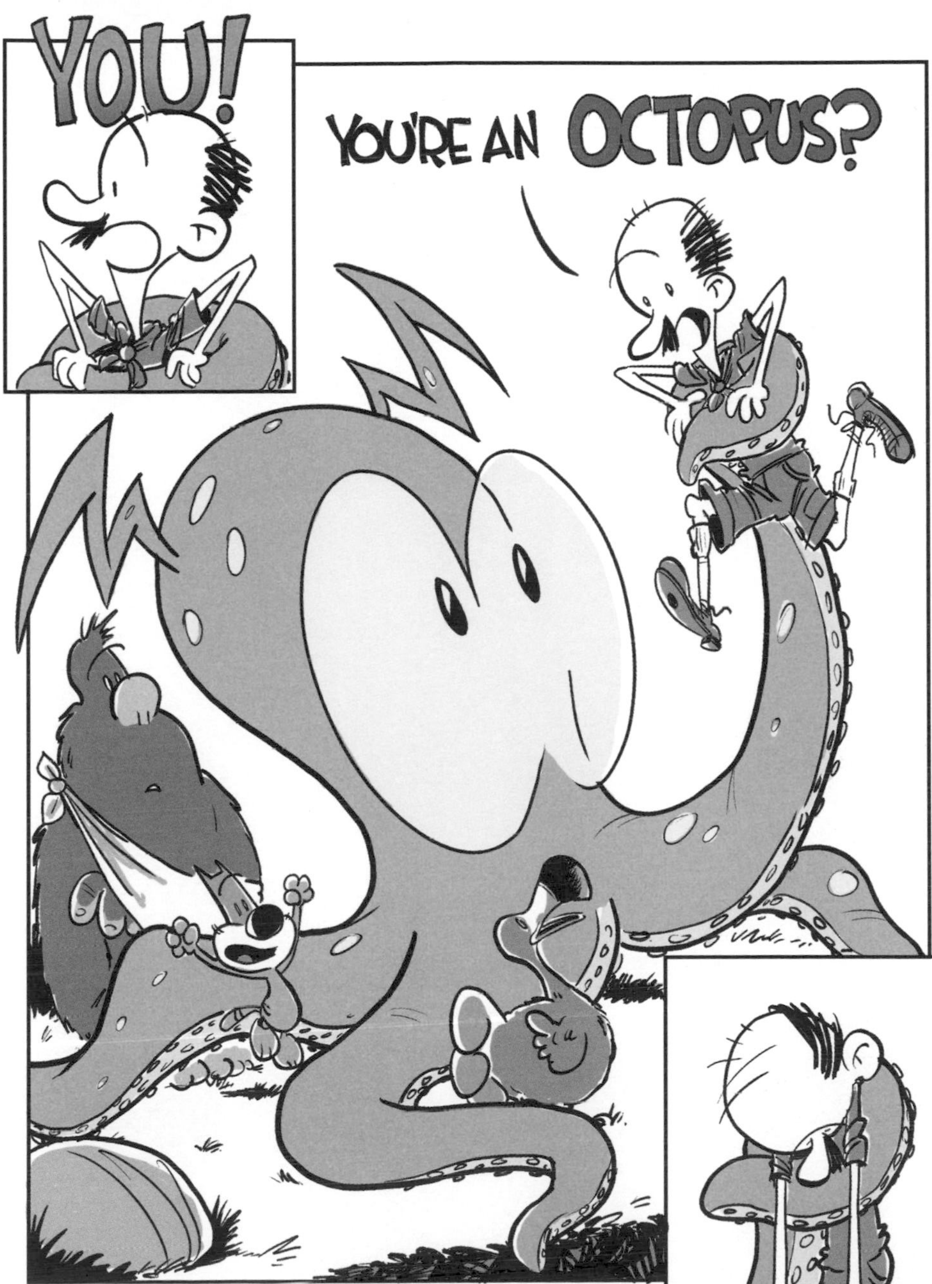
YOU!
YOU'RE AN OCTOPUS?

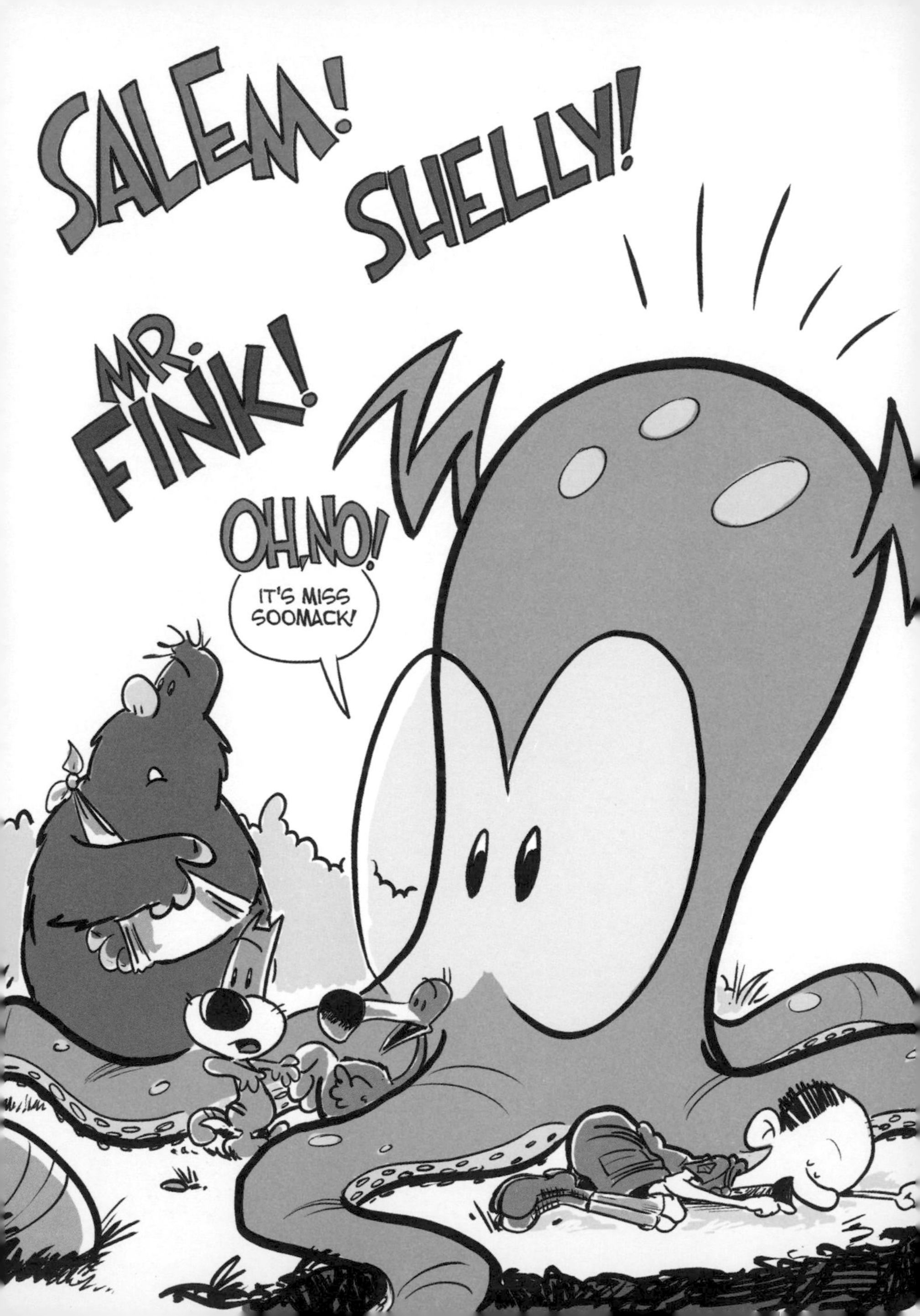
SALEM! SHELLY!
MR. FINK!
OH, NO!
IT'S MISS SOOMACK!

91

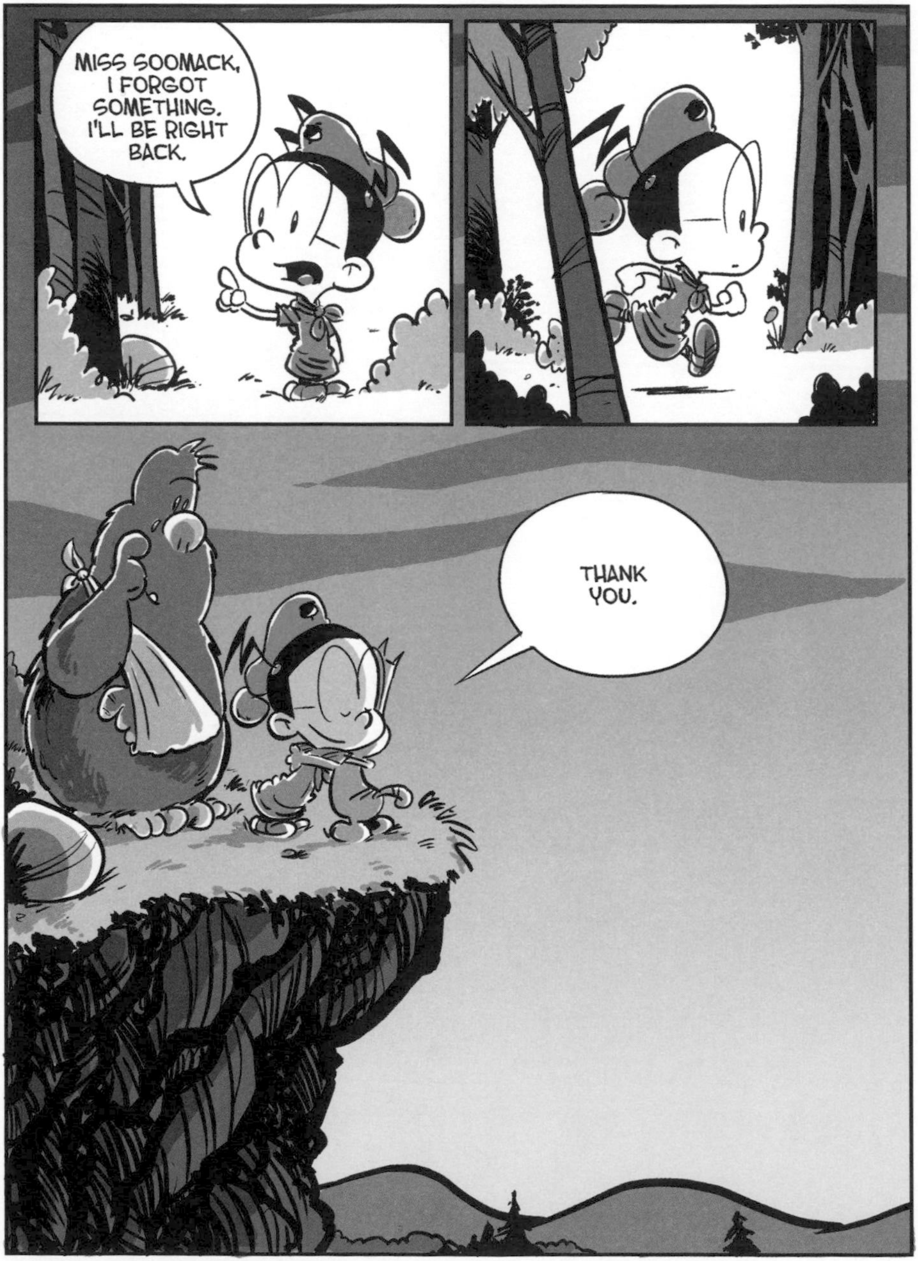
MISS SOOMACK, I FORGOT SOMETHING. I'LL BE RIGHT BACK.
THANK YOU.

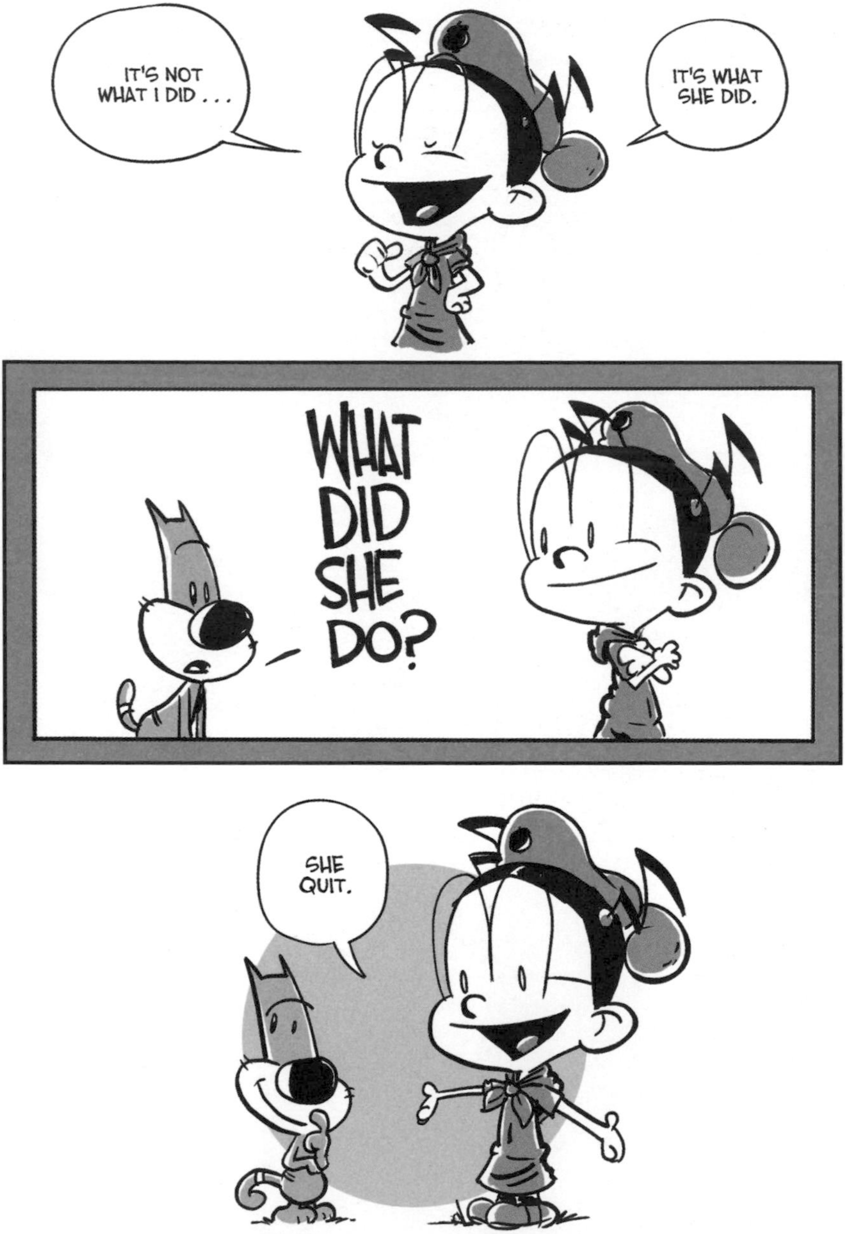
IT'S NOT WHAT I DID . . .
IT'S WHAT SHE DID.
WHAT DID SHE DO?
SHE QUIT.

Getting to KNOW FRANK CAMMUSO

FRANK LIKES
1. TRAVELING WITH HIS FAMILY
2. COOKIES (ALL KINDS)
3. DRAWING COMICS
4. PLAYING LEGOS WITH KHAI

FRANK DISLIKES
1. TUNA FISH
2. MAYONNAISE (ALL KINDS)
3. SHOVELING SNOW
4. CAMPING IN A TENT

FUN FACT: DID YOU KNOW...
THAT FRANK CAMMUSO WAS ONCE A BOY SCOUT?

SPECIAL THANKS TO ...

Ngoc and Khai, Kathy Leonardo, Nancy Iacovelli, Hart Seely, Tom Peyer, Maggie Lehrman, Charlie Kochman, Katie Fitch, Chad Beckerman, Morgan Dubin, Judy Hansen, and finally to all the folks who recommended I get a CINTIQ.

For more fun stuff about Salem and Whammy
check out my website at ...
www.cammuso.com